The Lightn

Producer & International Distributor
eBookPro Publishing
www.ebook-pro.com

THE LIGHTMAKER OF AUSCHWITZ
Naphtali Brezniak

Transalation from Hebrew: Bernie Mezrich
Contact the author: brezniak@gmail.com

ISBN 9798865298205

The Lightmaker
of
Auschwitz

*A WW2 Historical Page-Turner Based on
the True Story of a Holocaust Survivor*

NAPHTALI BREZNIAK

Contents

Translator's Introduction

"There isn't a novelist who can write about what happened,
No one can understand what happened,
You can't tell, you can't understand,
You cannot believe."

Moshe Brezniak

I met Naphtali, the son of Moshe Brezniak, in Tel Aviv at the Mezritch Memorial Society[1], a group preoccupied with a small ghost town in eastern Poland; their endless task is to preserve the memory of Jewish life uprooted by the Holocaust. My father Mordecai also mourned his family after fleeing from Mezritch, a sadness that spanned 35 years. Many survivors exhibit this unresolved attachment to their childhood hometown. Literature shows a good example in "Fateless" (also a movie) about a young Jewish prisoner who yearns to return from the concentration camp to Budapest, the city that actually betrayed him.

There were three towns in eastern Poland named Mezritch. No, this was not the home of the famous "Magid" who was credited with founding Hassidism. Rather, this Mezritch - Miedzyrzec in Polish, meaning "the junction between two rivers" (see Notables Section) - was a cosmopolitan center with

---

1.For a look at the Mezritch Memorial Society in Israel, follow the link to: http://www.mezritch.org.il

7

a secular Jewish majority, full of creative energy and universal curiosity. There were 18,000 Jews in 1939 but only 180 of them managed to survive the war, Moshe among them.

Here is my English translation of "The Birch Trees Stand Tall", Naphtali's record of Moshe's dictated accounts for the Yad Vashem Holocaust Testimony Series that was published in Hebrew in 2003. This book title honors his father's tenacity for survival while maintaining his humanity. The family name "Brezniak" (literally meaning "erect birch trees" in Polish) reflects Moshe's character. As the war broke he first endured a German POW camp as a defeated Polish soldier, survived the Mezritch Ghetto until deportation, and was then herded through many of the worst death camps. Amazingly, Moshe survived the entire nightmare through ironic luck and his ability to absorb loss, while somehow persevering until his release at the war's end.

After reading the Hebrew original three year ago, I endeavored to complete this English translation for a wider readership, including our overseas families. This project also honors my father Mordechai and his memories of Mezritch, where most of his large family perished[2]. The poignant stories he retold at the Shabbat table have come alive with Moshe's vivid descriptions, authenticity of detail, and honesty of emotions. By recalling still-born personalities that were annihilated in the war, both of these Mezritch 'orphans' revealed a familiar melancholia.

Although Moshe waited fifty years to open up, his stories are genuine, though morbid, obviously depressing and difficult to absorb; but they are also compelling. During my first reading a childhood dread chilled me again with an insecure feeling:

2. My father sadly left Mezritch before the war, never to see his parents or seven brothers and sisters again. Read his story in: **The Mezritch Bulletin No. 46 Sept. 2006**, at the link:
http://www.mezritch.org.il/Tribune-renumbered_low.pdf

had we been born several years earlier and in another continent the Holocaust may have been our reality too.

Translating and editing this book have generated these questions:

1. What kind of personality survived the World War II Holocaust?
2. Did a resourceful electrician who hid pliers in his ragged coat lining for the transport instead of diamonds have a better chance to survive?
3. Did a fair-play wheeler dealer smuggling abandoned goods to buy his way into the camp depot that sorted dead-prisoners' spoils extend his life?
4. Did building a bunker in the doomed ghetto, futile as that was, buy more time for his family?
5. Why did some German soldiers and police risk their lives by giving this prisoner one more chance, foolish as that was?
6. Can non-Jews admire this survivor's story, or imagine such a pervasive threat to their own family's race?
7. Would you or I have survived this Holocaust?

This chronicle is like a memorial candle for the dead that validates the experience of any remaining survivors, and it hopefully provides a beacon of hope to enlighten us from the darkness that has shrouded this tragic episode in the history of civilization.

Onward,

Bernie Mezrich
Tel Aviv

Preface

For many years would tell us about the terrible period. Shabbat mornings were dedicated to the stories. The stories penetrated into my being until I occasionally felt I had been there

In his last year, when Dad was 83 and still working, I decided to write down the stories. Dad told them and I recorded. After each story I entered the material into my computer and Dad would review the printouts. He didn't accept even the slightest variation from the truth. For example, if I wrote about a German officer when a regular German soldier was involved, he would insist upon a correction. This dialog continued as usual from Shabbat to Shabbat, his story, the printout and the editing.

In December of 2000 Dad was suddenly taken ill with an incurable disease. I had no idea how long we would be together. We never discussed the severity of his condition with him, but he knew.

One day I arrived at the hospital with pen and paper.

"Dad, we have plenty of time today." I said to him, "Start telling your story." and noted where we had left off during the last interview.

"Not enough time left for me?" asked Dad.

"Speak as if you don't have enough time." I said.

"But Mother suffered more than me." he said.

"Speak Dad, speak; I want to hear you."

And Dad, very weakened, started to speak. He spoke and spoke and spoke.

"If Dad could continue speaking nonstop he would be with us today." I told my sister several days later. Dad had such vitality when he told his stories. He turned the story into a reality of color, smell, motion, and sound. I'm certain that I missed much, but I hope that Dad's spirit, the strength he projected, and the bit of the philosophy that he allowed me to quote within his narration, will reach you too. **To remember and not to forget** was the motto of each interview.

Dad died on the tenth of January, 2001. That day I eulogized Dad and my best friend.

May his memory be blessed.

Napthali Brezniak

Prologue

How many souls does a person have? How many times does the Angel of Death circle above someone's head and then disappear? Perhaps simply, how many times can you be saved from certain death

- in war, and particularly during hand-to-hand combat with the enemy?
- as a prisoner of war, because of your being a Jewish soldier?
- as a prisoner of war, standing over the grave you dug for yourself?
- during the *actzias* in your city, with the luck of being at the right place at the right time?
- for no reason between the *actzias*, when you've been confronted by Schleiger, the butcher from Menschenschreck?
- on the death trains while going to the extermination camps?
- as a result of unforgivable disobedience and sins in the death camps?
- as a result of exhausting work: digging, putting down rail tracks or digging in coal mines?
- for smoking a cigarette in a German bunker during an actual air-raid?
- for just starving?
- from the British bombing of the transport train?
- from weariness, weakness and hunger during the death march?

when the order to kill you is thwarted for reasons unrelated to you?

This books provides partial answers, at best, to these questions and many more.

Growing Up

Six times my mother bore babies. Four sons and two miscarriages wasn't a bad accomplishment for a young woman of 28. I was born on the sixth of May in 1917, and about six months later, in December, Mother died. Her briefly endured illness brought her from Mezritch-Podalski[3] to the hospital in Warsaw, where she was also buried.

I never got an answer when I called out to "Mother".

My father, Judah, who was widowed, left me with the best substitute for a mother - a nursemaid. Father left Mezritch which brought him no joy after Mother's death, for his birthplace in Trevniki, a town neighboring Lublin.

A year after my mother died, Yachad Giverc, the daughter of a wealthy Lublin family who owned land in the Jozkavki region near Trevniki, became the step-mother to Naphtali, Zeev and me. An unwritten agreement between my mother's parents – from the Goldberg family – and my father divided the burden of education and care of the orphans between the two families. My brother Chaim, who was six, remained in Mezritch. The three of us went with Father to live in Trevniki. Yachad was unusually pleasant to us, her foster children. Nonetheless I couldn't make her my genuine mother.

---

3. The official Polish name of the is Miedzyrzec Podlaski. Mezritch is the Yiddish pronunciation that will be used throughout the book.

I lived in Trevniki for the first eight years of my childhood, rolling between two huge oil tanks in the yard between our house and the family store that sold petroleum and wood products near the municipal train station. My father, assisted by my oldest brother Naphtali, owned the franchise to sell petroleum products in Trevniki that he received from the Eichenbaum family residing in Lublin. This family controlled the most of the petroleum products in the region, and the local refineries also belonged to them.

The eight good years ended when my father's franchise was revoked because of cutbacks. The economic situation forced him to split up the family once again. In 1925 his three sons were sent to Mezritch, to Grandmother's house. The four daughters who were born to Yachad remained with them in Trevniki. Thereafter I saw Father very infrequently, only when he came to Mezritch for family celebrations. I never returned to Trevniki during my childhood.

For the next six years my brother Chaim became the dominant figure in my life. He was a father and a mother to me and I did almost everything to please him.

Our first conflict occurred when I completed grade school. Chaim insisted that I continue studying in the local gymnasia but I tended to emulate my father – wanting to be independent. Chaim, who understood the added value of studies, maintained his position. And because I only spoke Yiddish, he sent me to learn the local language, Polish, from Shprintza Zemel. Nonetheless, I didn't abandon my dream to be self-sufficient.

"I want to learn a profession." I tried to convince Chaim on one of the days I returned from the Shprintza residence.

"What do you want to learn?" Chaim asked, while still against the idea.

"Electricity", I answered.

"Why electricity?" he asked and from the strain in his words

I deduced that he believed his younger brother deserved a better profession.

"Why do you work in the Electric Company?" I was being stubborn.

Chaim didn't answer. Chaim didn't usually supply answers. He was very subdued, always seeming to be engrossed in something far away.

Being an electrician didn't appear to be a bad goal for me. The fact that Chaim worked in the local electric company only enhanced my ambitions. Also the light bulb, the radio, and the telegraph enchanted me. The future would prove me correct.

After a few days of indecision, Chaim honored my request and brought me to Meir Podolak. Meir, who was my brother's age, was known around Mezritch as a very talented person. At the age of 18 he received a government license to operate an electrician's business – an unimaginable achievement at the time. I became Podolak's apprentice, when I learned my first steps in the theory of electricity.

* * *

While working for Podolak I joined the *Hashomer Hatzair* cell in Mezritch. It was not only the socialism that attracted me, since Chaim had an influence as well. Chaim was a senior counselor in the cell, and his name was well known and even spread to the bigger cities. I had a very talented brother, and due to his command of Hebrew he was among those responsible for the newspaper, **Our World**, that was published by the local cell members.

Several months after I started my new life my brother Zeev moved out to Warsaw. He told us that he was going to try his fortune in the big city in textiles. But apparently he went there to evade the authorities; they wanted to ban him because of his political activities in illegal leftist organizations like the Communist Party. The separation from Zeev, who was closest to me in age and most involved in my life, awoke my desire to follow in his footsteps to Warsaw.

"What do you think about my going to study?" I asked Chaim.

"You're fed up with work?" he asked, and his eyes lit up.

"No", I answered. "I want to be a certified electrician."

"And where do you want to learn this profession?", Chaim wondered.

"In Warsaw!" I answered.

"Warsaw?" Chaim asked.

"Yes, in Warsaw." I answered. "Will you let me?" I added, without waiting for a reaction to my courage.

I thought of killing two birds with one stone: being close to Zeev and learning a profession.

"Give me time to think." Chaim said, and sunk into his thoughts again.

After several days a solution was found. The "ORT" school seemed ideal, since the studies would be paid for by the workplace that they had found for me. Living quarters remained a problem, but I overcame that, too, with initiative and daring.

* * *

Chaim had a friend in Warsaw, by the name of Mandelboim. Mandelboim's uncle had an electrical appliance store in Gizela Berema 9 Square. I worked half a day in the store and the other half I studied. The salary, which was modest, satisfied most of my needs – food, clothing, tuition, and culture. I didn't have enough for rent, so when it became dark I snuck back into the store and slept there. That's what I did every night for two years without the store owner, Mandelboim's uncle, being aware.

Zeev, who was supposed to be my patron in Warsaw, couldn't

support me; he could hardly make a living himself. Zeev was a member of the Communist Party that was illegal in the Poland of those days, and he would move and roam about constantly in fear of the authorities. Only rarely would I meet him secretly, in a different place each time.

Despite Zeev's considerable influence on me, I remained faithful to my Zionist views and joined the local *Hashomer Hatzair* cell. The cell was very large and lacked the family intimacy that characterized the Mezritch cell. It was so big that I only knew the members of my group.

* * *

In 1933 I completed my studies and returned to Mezritch, after a two year lapse in Warsaw – due to my lack of funds. I returned to work for Podolak, this time not as an apprentice but as a certified professional electrician, and I wasn't even 16 years. After several months of specialization I felt experienced enough and confident to take the next step. I asked Chaim to use his connections to get me into the local electric company. I sought more varied and more stable work, and wanted a more promising future.

The electric company and the Mezritch power station were owned by the Finkelstein family. The company facilities were located near the Jewish cemetery. The site had a huge generator that supplied the entire city, and there was also a lumber mill nearby, also owned by the well-to-do Finkelstein family.

My specialty was inspecting electric meters. According to the law, every meter had to be checked in the electric company's laboratory once in three years, and there was considerable activity involved in removing and installing meters at customers' homes. We were a team of two workers, a Polish lad by the name of Manchinsky and me. When we weren't dismantling or installing electric meters we were busy reading the usage data. Even though only 20 percent of the houses in the city were connected to the power grid, there was plenty of work.

Working in the electric company greatly improved my economic situation. The income was steady and relatively high. And so I suddenly found myself able to travel to Warsaw and when I wished, to see a performance or tour about. Occasionally, I went to Warsaw in the evening, saw a show and returned to Mezritch the next morning straight to work, even though the trip took four hours in each direction.

The theatre was my great love. Until today I remember well most of the performances that I saw and even some of the text – and this was 65 years ago: "War and Peace", "41", "Life Happens", "The Dybuk", "The Gold Patch", "On the Road at Night", the singer Sirutti's performance and many more.

In Warsaw I met Yaffa who lived in Otvochek and worked in the big city. Yaffa would buy tickets and we would go to the theatre together. After the show I would sleep in a hotel next to the bus station for the price of one zloty per night.

Once I arrived in Warsaw without arranging with Yaffa beforehand. I walked innocently down Genshe Street, a main street that drew many people to it. I stopped near one of the shop windows and, when I looked in, I saw her. I was certain that she was in the shop, and when I turned to enter, I saw that she was actually standing behind me. I still remember today the excitement that gripped me.

We decided to see "Shnay Coney Lemel", a performance put on by the Vilna Theatre. This time we didn't book tickets in advance.

"For this evening ?" the ticket agent asked as we reached the theatre entrance.

"Yes." we answered.

"Sorry" he said, "All the tickets are sold out weeks ahead of time. What, you don't know?", he added in amazement.

"Can I speak with the manager?" I asked.

The ticket agent giggled but agreed to call the manager.

"I came from Mezritch." I said to the tolerant manager.

"From Mezritch ?", he asked.

"Yes." I said, my confidence growing.

Mezritch was considered respectable even to culture seekers. Although the city didn't have its own theatre group, many of the important Polish theatre companies performed in the city's Olympia Hall before their premiere.

The theatre manager eyed Yaffa and me up and down and from right to left and then said, "Even though all the tickets have been sold, I'll guarantee that you shall see tonight's performance."

Yaffa almost fainted.

"I'll add two chairs in the aisle, if you don't mind."

We didn't care.

"If the city supervisors come to inspect," he added, "the responsibility is totally yours."

We could only thank him for his rare gesture.

The ticket agent didn't believe his ears when he was instructed to issue us with a pair of tickets, and mumbled something about the boss's good heart.

The show was wonderful, and no city inspection took place on that night!

* * *

On January 1937 I went for training (*Zionist hachshara*). My brother Chaim was exiled to Australia in the beginning of March because of his involvement with the Communist Party, a serious crime that was worth it to him, and like my brother's name – made him feel alive.

* * *

As a youth I spent most of my evenings with the *Hashomer Hatzair* cell. When I joined the movement I apparently did what my brothers expected of me: Chaim was a leader in *Hashomer Hatzair* and a member of the Communist Party, Zeev was an active member in the Communist Party, and I didn't disappoint them. At first I was in the Desert Sons class, and the following year I graduated to the Young Lions. I did the next two classes, Scouts and Advanced Scouts, during two years in Warsaw and I returned to Mezritch for the Adult class.

The movement's activities in the evenings, the weekends and in summer camps were similar to the activities that today's youth-movement members experience. The main difference was in the teaching of a firm and deep ideology: memorizing the "Communist Manifesto" was necessary to avoid disgrace.

The chapter on "Zionism" was also important, but the number of those from Mezritch who realized their Aliyah before the war was quite thin. It was good for us in Mezritch, very good indeed, and most of us saw our future there.

I, who saw my future in Eretz Yisrael, had to pass one more station in my course of professional training before making Aliyah. And so, upon becoming 20 years old, I told my family that I was packing everything and leaving for Rovna, for training by *Hashomer Hatzair*.

The packing was quick and without hesitation. I put all my possessions into suitcases – excluding two expensive shirts that I left in my Aunt Rachel's house at her insistence – and I arrived at the train station. I don't remember now if I was excited at the time, but I remember being determined. I felt good with the fact that right after my training, in only two months, I would satisfy my soul's longing – to reach Eretz Yisrael.

I traveled alone. Avraham Katz, my close friend, was already in Rovna, a fact that gave me a feeling of security in my travels to the unknown. I arrived in Rovna that evening. I left the heavy suitcases for safekeeping at the train station and walked to the training center. It was an old and ugly building, at one time a prison house that the authorities rented to the national leadership of *Hashomer Hatzair*. I reported to the secretary of the kibbutz (from now on training would be called "kibbutz") and told him that all my belongings were still at the train station. He calmed and assured me that the kibbutz would arrange to bring it here. What I was not told was that from this moment all of my possessions belonged to the kibbutz. I learned this quickly by myself.

"Why are you wearing my shirt and walking in my shoes?", I asked in surprise when one of the kibbutz members appeared before me.

"What is yours is mine!" he answered and smiled.

Behind him another kibbutz member appeared wearing my winter coat. "This is mine", he said.

I was shocked. I returned to the secretary and he revealed to me one of life's secrets: "A kibbutz is a collective and there is no private property. From the clothing you have brought we have decided to allow you to use one suit and a pair of shoes", he said. "And even these items will be shared by the group" he concluded.

I finally understood the basic principle – and didn't even dispute it - everything belonged to everybody. The kibbutz in Rovna, under the responsibility of Kibbutz Ein Hamifratz in Eretz Yisrael, numbered about 50 members. My first meeting with the kibbutz members shocked me. Resources were scarce everywhere. Most of the members went around in torn clothing and shabby shoes. Being skinny and pale was common. In the beginning I didn't understand why most of the girls remained in their beds in the morning and didn't go to work – that's why we came. Were they ill?

By the first evening I had already understood that about half the members were unemployed and supported by the other half. Our economic situation was awful. We were poor and hungry. The daily food budget was 22 cents per person, when a kilogram of bread cost 20 cents. The income was meager and the living expenses high: the electricity, telephone, and the abortions – yes, the branch of artificial abortions was highly developed in our kibbutz. The men and women members didn't exactly observe the "Tenth Commandment" – the watchman shall keep sexually pure. I finally understood...

The local Zionist Party in Rovna actually supported the kibbutz, but their resources were limited. There was also a generous Jewish family that had left their apple orchard for the kibbutz – the planting, the pruning and irrigation, and the picking was done by us. But the apples from this orchard never got to the market, since the hungry kibbutz members devoured them before they were even ripe.

The crowding there was extreme and occasionally we were forced to sleep two to a bed. One night I awoke with a fright when strange hands began stroking my body. "Why are you trying to remove my underwear?" I shouted at my bed-mate, who had a far-reaching interpretation of sharing and friendship. "I am still alive." I added. I wasn't aware of such things, but it seems that I was in the minority. How naïve.

The work dispatcher initially placed me as an electrician in the Culture High School building that was erected in the city. The local contractor explained to me that I was working for fees – the more work I did, the more money the kibbutz would receive. The challenge suited me and I worked at an insane pace. At the end of the day, when I came to collect my salary, he explained to me that he couldn't keep his promise and he paid me exactly what he paid the others. He got the output but I didn't get any fees.

In the evening I told the kibbutz-secretary that I was not prepared to return to that place because the contractor had manipulated and swindled me and it was also against my ideology – I, who came from a considerate home, could not grab work from the local Poles, most of whom were unemployed.

Consequently, I appeared for work at the lumber mill, very hard work that required great physical strength. The Polish laborers would roll the huge tree logs into the sawing machine and then we, the kibbutz members, would drag the cut boards on our backs and piled them on the other side of the building. At the end of the day our shoulders were disjointed. The Poles, who wanted to rest now and then, would stick metal into the wooden logs and the saw-blades would immediately bend or break, stopping the production line. Despite the intentional sabotage, the Poles received a higher salary than we did. No, the owner wasn't crazy, he was just anti-Semitic...

The heavy menial work damaged my shoulder. I transferred to another lumber mill where they sawed by hand, and the cut wood was sold for heat and cooking. There, too, my ideology intervened: the Jews who came to buy wood and remained there while the Poles were supposed to saw them, gave their addresses to the owner so that the kibbutz members could do the work in their homes. Although we profited, the locals, most of them almost starving, lost an essential means of livelihood. I couldn't face a Polish girl, who came with her laborer father to the saw mill in the hope of seeing him earn a bit of money to buy some bread – only to see her hopes crushed by socialist kibbutzniks. This fact bothered me so much that I asked the kibbutz-secretary to raise the issue at the member's meeting. The argument was lively. Three members joined my aggressive position, my friend Avraham Katz among them. But I remained in the minority. The dissent was so sharp and the ideological split so wide, that the secretary decided to invite to Rovna a senior activist from the national leadership. I remember our meeting with him as an especially traumatic night. A bitter ideological dispute broke out that lasted until the morning. A common understanding was not reached, and the competing positions became more polarized. By the end of that night it was obvious to me that my place was not with them.

But how do you leave when you don't have a coin in your pocket and what you brought to the kibbutz is no longer yours? I was out of ideas. It was forbidden to send or to receive letters or use the telephone, even collect. But since I didn't feel connected to the place anymore I decided to break the rules. I wrote to Chaim about my decision and asked him to send me 30 zloty for the trip home. "I'm leaving the kibbutz tomorrow." I told the secretary when the money arrived.

"Perhaps you can stay a few more days and help us?", the secretary pleaded with me. "We have new work and I am sure you could contribute and assist."

I wanted to leave on good terms and so I let myself be tempted into assisting the members in the factory that made wooden crates.

"You should deposit the money that you've received in the office." the kibbutz-secretary persuaded me.

"Why?" I objected.

"First of all, it's safer. Secondly, I personally guarantee that you'll get it back as soon as you ask."

I don't know why I believed him after my bitter experiences, but I deposited the 30 zloty with him that I had received from Chaim.

A few days later I decided that I had enough. I was determined to leave.

"I request my money." I told the secretary.

"Tomorrow", he said, "You'll receive the money tomorrow".

"I insist on getting it today!" I said. I assumed that something bad had happened.

"Tomorrow", he raised his voice. "Tonight there will be a meeting and tomorrow you'll get your money", he snapped.

"I want it now! I know that you haven't got it, right? You haven't got it!" I raised my voice.

He looked shocked.

"I haven't got it." he whispered, "I used your money for the general good. After all, you know what our situation is."

I knew that there was nobody and nothing to talk about. The "general" membership disgusted me. I felt cheated and angry. That man – the secretary – had simply robbed me.

I was embarrassed to turn to Chaim again and I searched for another way to earn the money for a train ticket. I met a local Jew at the wooden crate factory and we agreed that every crate that I made above the daily quota would count as mine and I would receive the money at the end of the month. By the end of the month I had collected enough money to travel to Lublin, where my eldest brother Naphtali lived.

Then, one day, disappointed and broke, dressed in torn clothes and shabby shoes while wrapped in a patched coat, I found myself knocking on the door of Naphtali's house in Lublin on the way to a new life. My Zionist ideology and the dream of Eretz Yisrael were both shattered to pieces.

The next day I traveled to Mezritch and I immediately appeared before Meir Podolak, the electrician. The salary I received for the first day of work equaled two weeks salary in Rovna. Private initiative beat socialism! I was disappointed. I was grateful to my aunt Rachel who had convinced me to leave the two expensive shirts with her in Mezritch before departing for the training. Those two shirts I could claim were entirely mine.

* * *

On the 21st of March 1939 I was drafted into the Polish Army and I returned to Mezritch exactly one year later on the 21st of March 1940. It was a particularly turbulent year: in the beginning of September the Germans invaded Poland and World War II broke out. After several weeks the unit I was serving with collapsed and I became a prisoner of war. At the time I did not know, no one could know, that the big storm was still approaching. When I was released from captivity the sky was still too clear. I returned to Mezritch with a letter in my hand from the local electric company promising me a position when I returned from military service.

A Soldier in the Polish Army

When I received the army's draft order I decided to let myself be drafted. In Poland the draft age was 21. Many Jews made every effort to avoid the obligatory service. But I decided to fulfill my duty.

On the 21st of March I was drafted into the infantry. My basic training, which was not very difficult, I did in Brisk. We learned to fire with mortar and heavy machine guns and to perfect sharp-shooting. The unit I served in had 200 soldiers and only three of them were Jews.

One day we were assembled into a hall for a lecture. The officer, who mounted the stage and began to speak, couldn't manage to impose quiet. The soldiers didn't pay attention to him. He turned to me: "Brezniak, isn't it true that the noise here reminds you of the synagogue?"

I rose from my place and answered: "When they ask for quiet in a synagogue you can hear the buzzing of the flies." I don't know where I found the impudence to answer the commander this way. They had drilled us to always answer: "Yes Sir!" no matter what was said.

The officer stared at me with penetrating eyes. Silence fell on the hall. I was certain that I would be summoned to a trial.

"Please be seated." he instructed me and began to lecture.

A few days later the commander left for vacation and

another officer took his place. We went out to train in hand-grenade throwing. I went into a trench and was given a practice hand-grenade.

"Do you see the target?" asked the new officer who didn't know me.

"I see it, Sir", I answered.

"Can you hit it?" he asked.

"Yes, Sir !" I answered with resolve.

"Do you remember the rules?"

"Yes, Sir !"

"Throw the grenade!", he boomed.

I made the motion of opening the safety pin and I threw the dummy grenade. I looked to see if I hit the target, and I realized that I had missed it by a few meters. I ducked my head, yelled "exploded" and waited.

"Did you hit it?" asked the officer

"No, Sir!"

"Do you want to try again?" he asked.

"Yes, Sir!"

"Run to bring the hand-grenade." he ordered.

I ran quickly and collected the fake grenade.

"Can you identify the target?", he asked me as I returned to the trench.

"Yes, Sir!"

"Throw the grenade!"

I threw the grenade a second time with all my might and saw that I had missed the target again. Once more I obeyed all the rules and I waited.

"Get out of the foxhole", the new officer ordered.

"Haven't you ever thrown rocks at Jews?" he asked with a scolding voice.

"A good citizen doesn't throw rocks at other citizens." I answered without delay.

"What did you say?", he asked.

"A good citizen doesn't throw rocks at other citizens", I repeated my words while inflating my chest upwards.

A higher ranking officer who witnessed the incident called the replacement officer. He whispered something into his ear. I was sure that from this moment, the new officer was acquainted with the fact that I was a Jew.

Every so often some soldiers would nickname me "Zhyd" (Yid). I never paid attention to them. The nickname went over my head. Since I never reacted to these jeers, they slowly disappeared from their vocabulary.

When our commander returned from his holidays, he suggested that I become his permanent personal servant. I immediately refused. I felt ashamed to be a personal servant.

"You are educated, you are an electrician. Why do you want to be a simple soldier?" he tried to convince me that it was worthwhile position.

I stood my ground and did not agree.

"Why did you say no?" I was asked by other members of the unit who were eager to become officer's servants.

"I want to be a regular soldier and to exercise like all other members of the unit." I replied.

The army maneuvers and training were not physically or mentally difficult; however, sometimes there was an interesting challenge. The greater the challenge, the more I exercised my intellect. I loved to use special talents that were probably hidden within me. I tried to be a good soldier and sometimes I gained special appreciation from the commanders. The number of free days that I received were my proof.

Once, I brought my bicycle from Mezritch when I came back to the camp in Brisk. The commander loved to use it frequently. Although I felt close to him, and I thought it was reciprocal, I never got relieved of my daily duties.

One day we were being trained in marching coordination exercises. The commander demonstrated by stamping his right foot during the march. I did not feel like obeying his order, and I stepped without stamping.

"Why didn't you stamp?" he asked me, while we were on the way back to the unit.

"My right leg is injured." I lied.

"Why didn't you inform me beforehand?"

"I forgot, Sir."

"Why didn't you inform me during the training?"

"We are not allowed to speak during the training, Sir."

"You are confined to the unit for the next 6 days." he sentenced me.

Three days later I won a very high marksman grade while hitting the target and the punishment was canceled.

The grade I received was high enough for me to qualify for a junior officers training course; however, my name was not registered.

"Why didn't they call me?" I asked the officer.

"Why do you ask, you know the answer." he replied and continued to walk.

One morning I was ordered to appear before the camp guard's officer in charge. Usually, that meant a court martial. I was not aware of any complaint against me. I was afraid that one of my friends from the underground communist party in Mezritch had sent me a letter, and this had been exposed by the military censors.

Pale and sweaty can describe the way I looked upon reaching the guards' headquarters. My heart was pounding strongly.

"According to the records," said the commander slowly, "You asked to serve as an electrician".

"Yes, Sir!" I answered and I tried to suppress the big smile threatening to spread on my face.

"At the end of basic training you will join the electricians' unit".

"Yes, Sir. Thank you, Sir".

At the end of the training I was posted to an infantry unit as a fighter.

I went back to my officer.

"Brezniak!"

"Yes, Sir!"

"What do you want?"

"Do you remember?"

"You mean the promise to become an electrician?"

"Yes, Sir!"

"Go to the administration commander!" he ordered, "Talk to him".

"I'd rather meet with you outside the base" the administration commander told me after hearing my request.

We decided to meet late at night in a coffee house belonging to a Jew in the nearby village. Although it was forbidden to leave the camp, I managed to slip away and arrived at the coffee house on time.

"Do you know the administration commander?" I asked the owner.

"Yes," he said, "What kind of business do you have with him?"

I told him.

"Without bribing him you won't manage to join the electricians' unit." he warned.

"How much?" I asked.

"50 zloty, at least."

"Where can I get such a sum of money?" I whispered, "It is a huge sum."

"Try to borrow it from a friend of yours" he answered sarcastically.

For this reason I never became an electrician in the Polish army. I felt that my dream was shattered. Only after the war did I understand that I was wrong to curse my destiny.

First Days of Horror

I saw the flashing of the cannons and heard the loud sounds of the first shelling of the Second World War on the border between Poland and Germany, close to the city of Bidgoshez, in the Tochola-Chuniza district. The infantry unit I served in had been posted there about one month before the war, performing guard duty next to the border as part of the unit's routine tasks. Our permanent base was in the area of Brisk. There was great tension in the air, however nobody thought about war.

The Polish Army considered me fit for two jobs: a flag-bearer during regular times and a sniper during emergencies and battle. This interesting combination was a challenging one. Being a flag-bearer was a special and desired job in the Polish army, however only a few got this assignment. Snipers had to go through numerous practice sessions and sometimes extremely rigorous training. There were tests at the end of each period and subject. My shooting accomplishments were among the highest in the unit, and I frequently received special leave for my achievements. When I was free I joined the unit training for heavy mortars. I hated the idleness and I loved to study. In order to become good at mortar firing one needed special technical skills and a good mind, and these requirements were very appropriate for me.

The daily schedule was routine along the frontier. We spent most of the day guarding the border from trenches. The

34

remainder of the day was devoted to digging and camouflaging new trenches. Very few hours were dedicated to rest and sleep. The German's front line was about 200-250 meters away from us. We were posted in an artificial water canal in the valley that buffered between the two armies, one of many water canals that crisscrossed this agricultural area.. We were so close to each other that at night we could easily hear voices from the opposite side.

Not far from our position were two bridges. Over the closer bridge, a metal railroad bridge, the train from Germany to Poland crossed everyday at 5:15 AM. North of this bridge there was a wooden bridge that served as a crossing for pedestrians, carriages and cars. However, this bridge was blocked from traffic. German civilians and farmers were the primary population in the border area between Poland and Germany. Polish families were in the minority, and hatred and contempt existed between the two nationalities.

Life along the front line was considered the worst period in military service, and for good reason. The food and regular supplies to the forward units were diverted to the supporting units further back, so not much reached the soldiers at the front. The guard duty was long. If at the base 2 hours was typical, at the front we guarded 5-6 hours straight, accompanied by the fear of moving in the dark. The numbers of soldiers qualified to guard declined each day. Therefore, the officers decided to replace guards only once during the night, compared to 4 or 6 times at the base. This duty was so difficult that many soldiers decided to escape and be jailed rather than serve on the front line. The infirmary was always filled and the number of those evacuated to the rear was greater than usual.

At dawn of September 1st, 1939 I was posted to guard. My position was the closest to the border and the railroad tracks. As happened every day, at 5.15 AM. I heard the train from Germany to Poland whistling as it approached the bridge. But after

35

this scheduled train I noticed that another train followed with cannons positioned on its open cars. Just before I managed to alert my fellow guards, or even dial the phone, I heard a huge blast. Apparently aware of the change, the Polish army had blown up the train bridge. Only later did I realize that since the Polish Intelligence knew about the coming war, the Polish Army had mined the bridge connecting the two countries with explosives. We, the soldiers on guard, had known nothing about it. Nobody had bothered to inform us.

I remember the image of the bridge blowing up as if it was happening today. The noise was ear-splitting, and the German train was forced to stop just before the destroyed bridge. Immediately following the explosion the Germans started firing light artillery at the border. A few shells landed nearby. It lasted for several minutes and then stopped. A tense quiet could be felt in the air. We thought that the Germans were doing regular maneuvers on their side of the border. Not one of us could even imagine that this was the first day of a world war.

Around 6.30 AM we received a phone order to immediately leave our position and to join the main unit. The distance was about 2 Km which we walked in the trenches. The rumors in the camp said that the German Army was doing regular maneuvers and the bomb shelling was probably a technical fault. The optimists among the soldiers were even happy since they believed that our tour at the front was over and now we would pack to return to Brisk, our permanent base. The contradictory rumors increased our confusion and the prevailing uncertainty.

For several hours we waited idly for some new information and orders. Later we gathered next to the headquarters to receive ammunition and canned food. Before managing to return to our tents and store our supplies we were called to return quickly and ordered back to the guard posts. The company commander ordered me to stay next to him and serve as a sniper or mortar specialist.

While close to the company commander, I heard orders being issued to the local civilians and to the soldiers. I learned that the army had ordered the farmers and Polish residents near the border to leave the area immediately. Meanwhile, we learned that many German civilians living in the area had placed large mirrors on their roofs as a sign to be identified and protected from aerial bombing by the German pilots. I realized that this event was a far cry from regular Germans maneuvers

In our forward guard post there was a company commander, his deputy, their personal servants, the radio operator, the runner, and myself. They brought plenty of food and even a case of vodka. They were sure of victory for the Polish Army. Some of them even got drunk.

At around 4 PM I saw four German tanks approaching our position.

"Can you hit them?" the officer asked me.

"Without a doubt, Sir", I answered.

"In the meantime direct your gun but don't shoot, keep it locked" he ordered. "I do not want to be exposed", he added.

I sprawled in the trench and directed my rifle. The tanks stopped, turned around and finally disappeared.

After sunset we were ordered to remain in the forward guard posts until morning. If the previous day we had set out to guard feeling quite complacent, now our legs barely carried us. There were scattered sounds of shooting, and tension in the air. Around midnight several soldiers joined us bringing food and drinks. As usual, two soldiers took the dishes and went down to the water canal separating us from the Germans to wash them. They hadn't returned by morning. With the first light of morning we saw their bodies in the distance, spread out close to the water line and obviously dead. Naively, we still thought that they were mistakenly shot by stray bullets. I'm not sure till today whether this speculation was wrong, since all night long we heard shooting and nobody knew who was shooting at whom.

I shot in order to kill for the first time in my life, that night between the first and second of September, 1939. On that night we heard horses galloping. We were sure that the Germans had infiltrated a cavalry unit that passed next to our guard post. We didn't see anything but we shot in the direction of the noise. The next morning we realized that these were horses running away from the nearby farm. The shooting in the dark of night exposed our position to the Germans, and we immediate absorbed a round of strong but short bursts of fire. We crouched in the trench, and none of the soldiers at our post was hurt.

Following sunrise, the sound of shooting ceased. The company commander sent one of the soldiers to the battalion headquarters to observe the situation. He came back informing us that the post was deserted. The company commander ordered us to retreat through the trenches to the headquarter camp. All the army posts along the way were abandoned. Empty cans and torn cardboards indicated that somebody had been there until recently. In the camp we met soldiers who told us that actually it had been decided to retreat from the border the previous night. Nobody could explain why we were forgotten at the front.

The remaining officers decided that we should move to the city of Chuniza. When we arrived we realized that local German civilians started to shoot and kill Polish civilians. At the entrance to the city we met what could be called "The Proud Battalion of the Polish Army". We were told that the battalion was preparing itself to attack the German invaders. We were asked to dig new personal trenches. When the digging was done an order came to move in the direction of the water canals that circled the city. It was hard to describe how we felt about leaving the trenches we had just dug. The Germans fired at our retreat. Our company commander was killed before we reached the canal-zone, where we hid within the entangled high bushes. Again, we were ordered to dig personal trenches and when the job was done we were allowed to rest within. I think I fell asleep immediately for several hours, or so it seemed.

At sunset, we were ordered to move to the nearby town. As I raised my head above the bushes I was shot at from three directions. The Germans had discovered our exact position and secretly surrounded us. Our only survival option was to withdraw into the forest, apparently the only place without Germans. We moved swiftly in the darkness towards the thick of the forest. Although the bullets were whistling by our heads, our casualties were fortunately minimal.

As we entered the forest we noticed food cans with German labels. We realized that we had entered an ambush. Our officer thought that if we crossed the forest in the direction of the railroad tracks we could join the rest of the troops who are retreating from the border. We decided to move on his order when suddenly the Germans started to shoot at us. We heard their shouts very close by. We were ordered to attach bayonets to our rifles. I never imagined that I would fight face to face, and kill a man standing only one meter before me. The total darkness prevented us from identifying friend from foe. Shots were fired from every direction. Our bayonets were stabbing human flesh. There was no way to know if you were stabbing a knife or bayonet into a comrade or the enemy. The screams were horrible. The fear was awesome. My heavy helmet rose up from my stiffened hair.

At the same time we heard officers shouting in both German and Polish: "Forward, forward!". After a cruel battle, we beat the enemy. The Germans withdrew, and we had only to gather our wounded and dead.

At sunrise we were ordered to assemble next to the battalion headquarters. There we were praised for the fighting spirit we demonstrated. The commander said that several soldiers had been killed, but the battalion managed to drive away the German invaders. Even though we had won, the commander ordered us to continue to withdraw. Within a few days we realized the harsh reality; although our units were wonderful fighters, the Germans were overcoming us and advancing and we were defeated and retreating.

The next two nights we battled hand to hand with the German enemy again. The uncertainty in this kind of combat raises many questions for the fighter: Did you really injure your enemy? Maybe you have hurt your best friend? I am certain that some of our soldiers were mistakenly hit by their companions. Maybe I was among those that made this serious error. I will never know for sure.

Our unit totally disintegrated on the fifth night of the war. All the officers were killed or disappeared and every soldier was abandoned to his fate. The next night about 15 soldiers gathered in one of the forests and we decided to march together towards Warsaw. We spent the night in the forest while taking turns guarding.

The following morning, being in the vicinity of a local village, I was sent to fetch water for the group. As I left the forest to pass a clearing, in the direction of the first houses of the village, I was discovered by a German pilot flying above me. The pilot dropped a bomb on me. Instinctively, I sprawled on the ground in the clearing. Luckily, the bomb fell about 10 meters from me and the enormous amount of dirt that was kicked up by the explosion totally covered me. I waited for the aircraft noise to fade, removed the pieces of loose dirt covering me and examined myself. Nothing had happened to me. I wasn't even scratched. I could not bring water for my comrades.

In the forest we survived on fruits and vegetables that grew in the small plots tended by the local farmers. But there wasn't enough, and every day soldiers were sent to the farmhouses to request food, with little success. One morning I went with another soldier to a remote farm house at the edge of the forest. I knocked on the door, it opened widely, and a well dressed elderly farm woman stood at the opening.

"May I have some food?" I asked her in Polish.

"I do not speak Polish", she said. "German, please", she added after a small delay.

I tried to say something in a stammered German. She did not understand.

"My daughter can translate from Polish" she said while inviting us to enter the house.

When she opened the door to the living room, apparently to call her daughter, I saw within an inner room an old German officer, dressed gloriously in his uniform with many medals on his chest. I alerted the soldier accompanying me by pointing my finger in the direction of the German officer. We both jumped from a nearby window and ran for our lives. The officer rushed to the window and shot at us with his pistol. He failed in his mission. This time we again returned without a scratch, but also without any treasure.

The next morning, another group of soldiers went to another village. When they returned, they told us that they had ordered a family whose house they had entered to supply them with food. This time, the order was fulfilled so we could quiet our hunger and quench our thirst not only with water but with milk as well.

Each night we progressed slowly towards Warsaw. During the day we observed from a distance that German units were moving about in the villages. It was obvious that we could not avoid Germans on our way, and only the forest was safe for us.

After several days of wandering around in the apparent direction of Warsaw we arrived at a clearing in the forest. There we saw four buildings that looked like school houses. A few s oldiers who were sent to scout the main building described upon their return that they discovered four girls who spoke Polish, and one German girl who was ordered by the Germans to guard the buildings. When we entered, the girls did not object. Quite the opposite, they were cordial and allowed us to shower and shave. When we finished washing – we had no change of clothes - they even served us breakfast. After days of wandering in the forest, we finally felt like we were really at home. The girls were generous and even invited us to remain for lunch. We had no reason to refuse. However, they conditioned our continued stay by helping them to collect potatoes from the nearby field. The deal was tempting. But our officer suspected a trap and decided to leave. Three other soldiers joined him and the rest remained, including me. I decided to stay. We felt very comfortable there. There was no better alternative. I did not notice that one of the girls left the place right after breakfast. I did not suspect a thing.

As a POW

As we waited for the promised lunch and enjoyed the relatively comfortable weather, we suddenly heard the noise of vehicles approaching the forest clearing. When we looked through the window we saw many German soldiers approaching us from everywhere, crouched for battle and crawling forward.

"Out! Raus!" They shouted at us after they recognized us. "Raus! Hands up! Hands up!"

We slowly exited, and stood along the wall of the building with our hands raised. German soldiers popped out from everywhere and circled us as they aimed their weapons at us. I didn't know what the German soldiers would do, nor what their orders were. My legs began to tremble. One of the girls who remained with us begged the German officer not to kill us, and he agreed. However, I was still overwhelmed with fear.

The soldiers, who saw that we all had our hands raised and that they weren't in any danger, came closer and circled us. The noise got louder and a big truck approached the central building. Several soldiers searched the other buildings to check if anybody still remained. They pushed us in the direction of the open truck and ordered us to climb in. At the rear of the transport I noticed a frightened civilian. He was a local Polish man whom the Germans had captured on the way to the forest clearing. He said that the Germans told him that they were going to kill him, and we had every reason to believe him.

The truck brought us to Bidgoshez, a nearby town, into a camp that once served as a big stable for a Polish cavalry base. Inside there were many Polish soldiers and civilians. The civilians, I later discovered, were from the nearby city and other local villages. The three soldiers and the officer who had left before us were also there. They were caught minutes after they fled into the forest. They sat us in rows. We were forbidden to get up, and whoever wanted to use the bathroom had to raise his hand. We didn't receive any food or water the whole day. Late that night several German soldiers arrived and stood around us. In the dim light I saw that each one of them was holding a sack.

"Don't move!" we were ordered several times and I didn't understand why. Then suddenly, all at once, they started to throw pieces of bread at us.

* * *

"Imagine for yourself a starving person with a fresh piece of bread so close, not allowed to reach for it. Just imagine," Dad said.

* * *

September is the month of Jewish High Holidays - Rosh Hashana, Yom Kippur and Sukkot. During one of the holidays, while we were still in the stable, I saw a group of German soldiers abusing several Jews who were caught praying in the local Synagogue. They were brought to the camp and were ordered to change their positions all the time: to lie down, to get up, and to jump, as the Germans shot at them from time to time. Later, they were led to the further side of the camp but I don't

44

know what happened to them. It was the first time in my life that I witnessed such cruel abuse of a human being, a person of my faith. Abuse for its own sake. And I didn't know then, no one knew, that compared to what the future promised, this was only child's play.

* * *

The day after the holidays a Gestapo officer arrived and started calling names from a list that he held - Zukerman, Birenbaum, Finkelshtein – pausing a few seconds between names. He was looking for Jews from the local community. We discovered afterwards that German civilians from Bidgoshez informed the German soldiers that on the eve of the war the local Jewish community had boycotted German products. The names that were called belonged to the community leadership committee. No one responded: the committee members weren't there. They had escaped before the fighting started, knowing what abuse the German wringer intended for them.

Suddenly, in the heavy silence I saw a hand rise. It belonged to someone related to the committee who hadn't fled, because his mother had died on the first day of the war and he remained for her burial. "I am a Jew from the town," he said. The German signaled him to approach and continued to read names, but nobody else volunteered. At the end of the process he was taken away, never to be seen again. I don't know his fate.

Staying in the stable was unbearable. I searched every possible way to leave the place. Going to the toilet quite often, whether necessary or not, made it possible to move somewhat my cramped, idle muscles. Each time I returned I had to sit in a row, not always in the same place. Eventually I tried to sit by the gates to see, and perhaps to understand, what went on outside.

Sometimes, several German soldiers would arrive escorting civilians. It appeared as if they were looking for someone in the rows. When discovered - he was taken outside and never seen again. It turned out that the German civilians blamed the Poles for injuring them and even for killing their relatives. A death sentence without trial was the only verdict for anyone suspected of harming a German citizen.

One morning some German soldiers appeared, wanting to draft POWs for work. Better to do something, I thought to myself, and I volunteered. Basically I jumped at the opportunity, and it really was an opportunity. The Germans took us to the camp gates in order to unload bread from trucks. The work was easy and satisfying. The next day I sat closer to the door in the hope of being called again for similar work. Indeed, the Germans came, this time at noon, looking for a group of POWs to do work. I volunteered immediately. The smell of bread seduced me.

This time we were brought to the center of town. The distance from the camp implied different work. Indeed, it was different! We were instructed to dig under the tombstones where civilians and soldiers had been buried, some who had been killed in battle and civilians who had been killed by neighbors of the other nationality. Poles killed Germans and vice versa. For us, it was only dead bodies that we were ordered to gather; their nationality did not interest us. The bodies were in advanced decay and the stench was unbearable. We buried the bodies in a plot near the cemetery. The Germans who escorted us had special masks with special filters. We were not allowed to cover our noses.

Local German civilians recognized us by our dull uniform: "Those Polish soldiers killed our families!" some of them shouted to our guards. When they were ignored, they pointed at us trying to convince the Germans that we, the soldiers, were responsible for the recent slaughter of their relatives during the first days of retreat. The stench, and the fear that the Germans would believe the civilians, followed us all that day. But at the end of the day a surprise awaited us. One of the civilians, from among those responsible for our activity, invited us to an unusual meal whose menu included fried pigeons. Did he give this as a compensation for our unusual job? Even with twenty years of hindsight I don't know if the work equaled the desert. At night we returned to the camp.

On September 15th I was still a humiliated Polish soldier retreating into oblivion on his way to Warsaw. Looking back, realizing what followed these POW days, perhaps this was an experience I would later miss.

* * *

The Germans transferred prisoners, including me, to build and fix the road leading from Bidgoshez to Warsaw, work that lasted about one month. We were attached to an engineering unit whose officer wasn't particularly young. He picked me as the translator since I spoke Polish fluently and understood some German. I knew I was the only Jew among forty men. Luckily, the camaraderie of the soldiers overcame the natural anti-Semitism of these people. Those soldiers who knew me and that I was a Jew never uncovered my nationality.

One day, while working on the road, a German newspaper rolled by me. Although it was hard for me to understand I learned that ten days before the war broke out Germany and Russia signed the Ribbentrop-Molotov agreement. This divided their domains of influence in Eastern Europe. From what was written I understood that my home town Mezritch fell into the hands of the Russians. According to this agreement the Wisla River that crossed Warsaw would serve as the border between the two countries. I was happy about that. I found out later that Mezritch had been captured in the beginning of September by the Germans, yet was handed over to the Russians according to this agreement. My friend Avraham Blushtain was even nominated to be the mayor by the Russian authorities. However, the Germans broke the agreement by the end of September and captured Mezritch for the second time. The Bok River, passing east of Mezritch, then marked the border between Germany and Russia, but this was also temporary.

At the end of the month we were brought back to the stables in Bidgoshez. There we were told that 40,000 civilians had died since the beginning of the war. Most of them were executed by the Germans who blamed them for harming local German civilians before the fighting and when the war began. There were no trials, just wholesale executions.

* * *

"The Germans are freeing the prisoners of war to return home" was the rumor I heard a couple of days after returning from forced labor on the road. Indeed, the next day prisoners were freed and the atmosphere changed somewhat. But by that evening it was announced that the releases were suspended, probably because some of the POWs who were freed had gotten drunk and killed four German soldiers at the train station.

That same night another rumor circulated: all the Jews were being released. Towards the evening we were all lined up in the assembly field. "All Jews are requested to move to the left side of the field", it was announced over the loudspeaker. I knew that there were about 10% Jews in the Polish army, so I wasn't surprised to see many Jews move to the left side of the field. I had a bad feeling. Why were they only letting the Jews go free? In the Polish Army there had always been a certain level of anti-Semitism, but I never witnessed the separation of Jews from others. Why were they doing this? I questioned myself. The order seemed suspicious. Faivel Farbman's brother stood next to me in the line. "I don't intend to move to the left side," I told him. "If and when I get caught, I'll explain that I didn't understand the order." I elaborated quietly. Yesterday I was used as the translator and today I didn't understand a word. "If they really release the Jews, I will say I didn't understand." I added. And if they don't release them, I thought to myself, that's good enough. We will see where fate leads me. Faivel's brother stepped left.

"Why aren't you going to the left?" asked one of the Polish soldiers who knew me and my identity.

"Why aren't you joining your Jewish brothers?" he asked me again when I didn't answer. I understood that he could point me out so I said: "I am just like you, a captive Polish soldier". I took advantage of the commotion and stepped away from him. Again I felt my heart pounding strongly.

After the line-up we went back to the stables. The Jews who moved to the left side of the assembly field were taken to a distant part of the camp.

I couldn't sleep that night. All these strange, unusual thoughts arose in my mind. If they truly released the Jews, I had lost. And if not, where did they take them? I had no answer. Before dawn I sat in the rows again. I raised my hand and asked to use the toilet. I walked slowly looking for someone to supply information about the fate of the Jews. When I got closer to the bathroom I noticed someone who appeared to be Jewish.

"Are you a Jew?" I asked him in Polish.

"Go away!" he answered and quickened his pace.

"Your accent betrays you", I tried to reach him. "I am a Jew too", I didn't leave him.

"Don't bother me", he answered trying to escape.

"You look like a Jew", I said in Yiddish getting closer to him.

"What do you want from me?" he answered in our mother tongue. He only relaxed when the nearby bathroom building hid us from view.

"Maybe you know the fate of the group of Jews from yesterday?", I inquired.

He hesitated and looked in every direction before saying: "I am a nurse in the base hospital". He paused and added: "All the Jews were taken into the hospital's cellar near the sick room where they were exterminated".

"Are you sure?"

But there was no one to ask anymore. The nurse disappeared into the labyrinth of the bathroom.

This is fate. A moment's decision and I am still alive. This time luck played in my favor, but not for the others. I thought about my friend Faivel's brother.

The next day we were taken to a transition camp.

* * *

The morning of October 20th, 1939 could be described as a black morning. The sky was gloomy, and dark clouds covered the heavens in all directions. The rain pelted down on the roof of the hut and the whistling wind didn't let up. The lightning flashes dispelled the heaven's darkness and the thunder and echoes rolling from one end of the world to the other reinforced their dreadful effect. Nothing could light up that morning.

We were 12 men in the enormous shack, all Jewish soldiers who fell captive to the Germans as POWs during different battles. I didn't know any of them. Destiny gathered us together in the corner of the shack, where sawdust covered the ground the building was built on. The extinguished fireplace was the only prominent item in its center.

I cuddled up in the gray army blanket. I could not detach from the event that bothered me since the day before.

What forced me to raise my hand and confess that I was a Jew, I pondered. I had always succeeded in these kinds of selections before. It was clear to me that whoever was identified as a Jew was killed one way or another. I knew that no Jew was saved, whether he was from Bidgoshez or a Jewish soldier in the Polish Army who fell captive. I understood that there was

50

only one judgment for Jews - death. Then why, of all things, did I raise my hand yesterday when the German officer asked if there were more Jews in the group, I wondered uselessly. I, always reasonable, cool-tempered and clear thinking, was hurt. How could I be tempted? I could easily have gone on playing the Pole - some even mistook me for a German - blond hair with light colored eyes.... It all collapsed the second I raised my right hand. Although it was only for a split second, the hesitant movement had caught the German officer's eye and he ordered me to join the Jewish group. It had all happened so fast, and with a commotion that characterized the German approach.

We had arrived the day before at the transition camp and were brought into a big hall where the POWs were divided into groups of 100 people, we undressed and were taken to the showers. While the ice cold water washed our bodies, a couple of SS soldiers entered the showers. They passed quickly among the bathers, and recognized four Jews among us. A Jew who turned his back at that moment was saved. Those four Jews were taken violently out of the shower, made to stand on stools in the center of the room and commanded to sing "Ha-Tikva" loudly. Although I was exposed to humiliation as a POW, this experience was horrifying.

After we got dressed and were made to stand in rows outside the shower, a senior German officer arrived who spoke Polish. He passed between us, Polish and Russians soldiers who fell captive, stared at us and said in Polish: "All the Russian soldiers[4] will soon be released. All the Polish soldiers will die".

So simply, my fate was sealed with the fate of the other Polish POWs. This time I was certainly on the side sentenced to death.

Suddenly, to everyone's amazement, one of the soldiers took three steps forward, as we were accustomed to do in the army, and said: "What is my fate if I am a Jewish soldier from Gal-

---

4. Editor's Note: he probably meant Polish Soldiers that lived in the new Russian Zone, according to the Ribbentrop-Molotov agreement.

izia?" The problem definitely seemed very complicated to the soldier; he truly didn't know where he belonged. Did he belong to the Polish group which was sentenced to death, or to the Polish-Russian group which was sentenced to live? Or maybe to the Jewish group whose fate he didn't know, thinking his friends were on there way to freedom.

The German officer was surprised. He looked at his presence, examined the Jewish soldier derisively and ordered him to stand aside. Then he roared in Polish: "Are there any more Jews here? Jews? Jews?" That sudden roar in Polish shocked me. My right hand started to rise against my will, like it was separated from my body. My hand rose and I immediately pulled it back down. My raised hand disturbed the absolute order that prevailed among the rows, and caused me, for an instant, to stand out. Immediately, without a moment's hesitation, he directed me to join the other Jewish soldier. Being petrified I walked towards him. I was in shock because I had failed. Up to now I had managed to hide my origin since I was blond and had blue-green eyes. But this time I didn't. The Jewish soldier who I was approaching didn't understand why I, just another Jew and not from Galizia, was joining him.

After the morning assembly both of us were taken with our hands raised to hut number 401, a huge shack that could hold hundreds of people, but only 12 of our countrymen were there. Some were caught in the showers and some were turned over by informants. And myself.

The German officer who was in charge of us craved respect and he found it in quantity in hut number 401. No one could stop him. He was responsible for 12 Jews. One of them was an officer in the Polish army – but a Pole and a Jew, more accurately - Yehudon, untermentsch, subhuman.

"I will discipline you!" he said after entering the hut. He nominated the Jewish Polish officer to be in charge of the group, which meant that he had to know every moment how many men were in the shack, how many left to the bathroom and to say it loudly to the German. Then he added a series of drills on how to salute to Hitler with a sharp shout "Heil Hitler!" The instructions lasted several hours until he was satisfied. We didn't mind the training, the movement, just doing something. Truthfully it made us giggle, and when we were by ourselves it was something to laugh at and ridicule.

At night the German led us with raised hands to the kitchen where each of us received about 100 grams of moldy bread and coffee. He called it coffee. Our sense of taste reported something diluted, tasteless and cold. We spent the frozen night on the sawdust that was spread on the ground and we cuddled up in an army blanket that we received from him earlier.

On that black morning of October 20th no one had to wake us up. When the officer arrived we were already up. David from Warsaw had already managed to finish his morning prayers and we served as his passive Minyan (prayer group). Zvi-Hirsh, also from Warsaw, tried to endear us and clown around or use black humor to somehow lighten our troubled psychological state. He liked imitating the German officer which made us laugh. Through the open window we noticed the German officer approaching the hut. The Jewish-Polish officer hurried to organize us in rows and waited for the German at the entrance. As he approached, wrapped up in his cape against the rain and the wind, he saluted and shouted "Heil Hitler" and was answered in kind, and immediately afterwards we saluted in unison as we had learned the day before. Since we weren't ordered to repeat it again, we understood that we had passed the test. It wasn't an exercise.

The German signaled two men in the group to come with him and for the rest of us to remain in the shack. As if there was someplace to go. Fifteen minutes later, they came back with wheelbarrows filled with shovels and picks, a shovel and a pick for each prisoner.

"What is there to do at such an early hour when a storm is raging outside"? Zvi-Hirsh whispered.

The German, who didn't hear the question, had ordered us to completely undress.

"Another shower"?, whispered Zvi-Hirsh.

We took our off our clothing slowly.

"Faster, faster", "Schnell" ordered the German, when our slow pace annoyed him. I laid my clothing neatly on the sawdust and hid my shoes under one of the logs in the corner. When we finished undressing in the brutal cold, we were each given a shovel and a pick-axe and then ordered to follow the German officer outside the shack.

Until today I can't forget the surrealistic scene of a dozen naked Jews stumbling after a German officer wearing a cape in the pouring rain, with a shovel on their right shoulders and a pick on their left. Leaving the cold, yet sheltered shack was insane. The freezing cold and the rain that we were suddenly exposed to stopped our breaths. We tried to bend to protect our bodies, but the roaring of the procession leader inhibited our reflexes. We walked as upright as we could, almost marching, through the trees of the young woods, in almost total darkness. We didn't even know in which direction we were going.

After several minutes we arrived at the columns of light shining from the spotlights along the camp fence. Before the German spread us along this fence, two meters apart, he said: "Each one is to dig his own grave", and he drew a rough outline of a grave. "The digging is to be parallel to the fence," he said. "And I will check you," he added after looking at us. "Whoever stops digging will be shot on the spot", he screamed and left. Luckily he didn't limit the time. Perhaps he did, but none of us knew. The instructions were short and he disappeared.

Suddenly the forest was filled with the sound of pick-axes trying to tear open the root-entwined ground that was most difficult to dig up. After only a few minutes, David from Warsaw, who was very religious, stood next to me and asked me to say "Shma Israel". I didn't refuse. And so I found myself, a non- religious Jew, standing on the morning of October 20th 1939, conspicuously naked before God, with a pick-axe in my right hand nearby my grave in the making, with David's hand atop my head as a yarmulke, saying the prayer "Shma Israel" out loud. What went through my mind during those moments? It's hard to say. Only this I remember – being furious with myself that I had brought this fate upon myself with one unnecessary movement. And who could I complain to?

The German occasionally came and went. He expressed his dissatisfaction with our slow progress by firing shots in the air. But he still didn't aim his pistol at us. One time, between his appearances, I heard Zvi-Hirsh advise us to dig slowly and live a couple of more minutes in this world...

Time passed. We no longer felt the endless rain and the strong wind. The vapor emanating from our bodies was clearly visible. Every breath covered our faces in a white mist that quickly evaporated.

I don't remember how deeply I dug during those three hours, but the officer's appearance and his order to suddenly stop digging broke my routine.

This is the end. I told myself. Now, he will simply stand us over the edge of the hole and shoot each one of us. I decided to stand erect, I don't know why, perhaps as a kind of final protest against the German who would take my life, or maybe to enter into the next world proudly. However, the German had other plans for us. He ordered us to take our tools and as before, we walked back with him towards the shack.

"Snack time," whispered Zvi-Hirsh.

Actually, he wasn't far from wrong. Without knowing why we returned to shack number 401, naked of course, but in an orderly fashion carrying our personal tools.

"Get dressed quickly!" The German shouted. "I will be back in ten minutes." and he turned and left.

"Someone has been here." I heard one of the group say. Indeed, my clothing had disappeared. Probably other prisoners had exchanged their clothing with ours, or they were just taken. Somehow we covered our nakedness, finding only my shoes under the log where I hid them.

The officer returned – the upraised "Heil Hitler" was repeated again - and marched us in a row, with our hands up, of course, and to our surprise – in the direction of the kitchen. Only there he was nice enough to tell us that he had to sustain us according to camp rules. And food had arrived for us. The well known need for German order saved our lives this time.

When we arrived, we saw long lines of other prisoners, POWs and civilians, waiting to get food. The German officer ordered some prisoners near the food counters to leave the area, not to mix with the Jewish criminals. Everyone moved without a word. Some even cursed us. The German ordered the food dispatchers to give us portions filled with pig meat, and marched us back to the shack, this time with only our left hand raised as a sign of surrender.

David refused to eat despite his gnawing hunger. This infuriated the German. He had never eaten and would never eat pigs' meat. He preferred to die from a pistol whipping by the German, but pig would not enter his mouth. David won this time, he stayed alive. He didn't let pig's meat enter his mouth despite the severe beating he endured.

* * *

The morning's abuse finished with drills and "Heil Hitler" salutes that we had become excessively good at. Towards evening the reason behind this demonstration became obvious to us. Representatives of the International Red Cross were about to visit the camp – to inspect prisoners of war. The German officer delegated cleaning tasks and had us straighten our clothes to put on a perfect show before these representatives.

At exactly at 6 PM we saw the group from a distance. Leading the group was a very high ranking German officer. The civilians from the Red Cross each wore an identifying band on their right arms. Behind the group were several more German officers and soldiers. As the honorable procession got closer to hut number 401 the German officer ruling us shouted "Heil Hitler" and saluted with an upraised arm.

"Heil Hitler!", repeated the Jewish-Polish officer who was appointed as our leader, just as he had learned.

"Heil Hitler!" we all roared after him.

Glancing from the side you could see the satisfied look on our German officer's face. "I've succeeded.", he probably thought to himself.

The punch he got in the face surprised us too. The senior German officer's shouts echoed in the hollow shack and throughout the whole camp. He explained to the officer controlling us that Jews were prohibited from uttering Hitler's name at all, especially as we pronounced it. Only a special population was honored to do so.

The inspection never took place, but who really cared. We came to realize that sometimes, seldom maybe, there is justice in this world. The man who made us dig our own graves in the morning had been totally humiliated in front of us, and by one of his own countryman.

The public humiliation ceremony completely changed the German officer. His aggressiveness towards us suddenly turned into positive energy. At once he tried to be our "friend". He told us that he was a reservist who had been called up to military service when the war broke out. Before the war he had been in divinity school. Hitler ordered the closing of all such institutions and the students were stationed in different units.

For the next couple of days he would lecture us about his faith and belief. "Each nation needs to be punished at one time or another," he said as a matter of fact. "You, the Jews, are being punished now, and we, the Germans, will be punished afterwards".

To pass the time he would ask us questions about history and Judaism, and he even tried to instigate arguments between us. He had a clear understanding of the difference between Judaism and Christianity. He was versed in the Bible and in sayings like "You kill the best of the Nations".

In the period following the Red Cross visit he spent more and more time among us, to argue about anything in the world, and even compared us favorably to the Poles, whose only interest was food, food and drink. "With the Jews you can have conversation," he used to say.

One day he brought us pre-printed postcards in order to describe our situation to our families. We could also report that more letters would arrive when we had settled in a permanent base. Actually we didn't write anything on the postcard except the address. We marked X in the appropriate place.

* * *

The days that followed in the transit camp were spent unloading processed wood from train carriages and arranging them in piles on flat areas nearby. There were thousands of prisoners in the camp and it was very easy for anyone to avoid work. The Poles complained about us to the Germans and accused us, the Jews, of shirking from work. The Germans, as a response, watched us very carefully and we were forced to work very hard.

In time the number of Jews increased. The Germans

brought POWs to the base from all the fronts, and among them were Jews.

One of the strange incidents that I remember from that period is that all the prisoners decided to grow beards. After several days we all had beards. This was really an unusual sight. The Germans, who understood that this was a form of protest against the captivity, immediately ordered us to shave. I don't remember how and where we found shaving blades; perhaps the Germans supplied them to us. But the following day no bearded POW could be seen.

Occasionally a Polish soldier died in captivity from a disease. There was no epidemic outbreak, but these things happened. The funeral seemed absurd and humiliating. It lacked respect. Friends took the body in a wheelbarrow and buried it over the fence, just like that. Once, when we watched such a funeral, somebody asked how we would behave if a Jewish soldier died. Indeed, the day arrived when a Jewish soldier died. After a short discussion we decided, a few friends, to arrange an orderly funeral. We tried to escort the dead man on his last journey in the most respectful way we could. I remember we laid the body on a stretcher built from boards and walked behind it. On the other side of the fence we dug a grave and buried him respectfully. Upon the grave we placed a Polish Army steel helmet that someone found in the vicinity and a Star of David nailed together from wood.

One cold night, in December or January, we were ordered to fetch wood for the fireplace installed in the shack where we stayed. The log warehouse was about 5 kilometers from the shack. We walked in the heavy snow and freezing cold towards the warehouse, where we saw several piles of wood. We innocently approached one of the piles, and loaded wooden logs on our shoulders, each one as much as he could carry, and slowly returned to the shack. As we approached the camp gates a German soldier appeared and told our officer in charge that we had taken logs from the wrong pile. That same night we were forced to replace the logs. We returned to the shack only after we had taken wood from another pile nearby the first supply, identical to it.

The POW camp where we stayed, originally regarded as a transit camp, was redefined as a permanent base. I spent about 5 months there. Despite being Polish soldiers, POWs, we were beaten and abused much more by the Polish soldiers than by the Germans officers and soldiers guarding us. From there, only the Jews were transferred to another camp whose name I don't recall; we remained there about another month.

Last Days As a POW

The new POW camp that we were transferred to was within a German Air Force base. Two important ingredients existed at this base: easy work and excellent food. And to our great surprise, whoever worked could shower at the end of the day. A shower at a POW camp - this was just unbelievable! The attitude towards those prisoners who worked was reasonable. However, it's worth remembering that we were a group of Jewish POWs, a fact we were reminded of frequently.

As usual after work every day the guards distributed a soap bar and towel to each one of us. We showered as usual and when done returned the towels and soap to the German officer. As we turned towards the dining room the commanding officer assembled us together and said: "I cannot believe that you are doing this to me".

Silence prevailed. I did not understand what he meant.

"Why are you doing it?" he asked in wonder, and immediately continued: "I gave you 100 towels and 100 soap bars, and you gave me back 100 towels and 99 bars of soap".

The uninterrupted silence lasted for several seconds.

"I cannot believe", he said, "I cannot believe that Jews would do this".

No one moved. We waited tensely for our punishment.

"This time I forgive you". The officer muttered.

He could easily have ordered the kitchen to deny us food or punish us in some other way. But he decided not to, nor did he demand the lost soap bar's return.

* * *

The unbelievable happened. My first letters sent from the transit camp actually reached the family in Mezritch. Confirmation appeared when several packages containing dry bread arrived from my family, exhibiting my brother Zeev's signature in plain view.

One day in March the usual morning assembly ended with the command: "All Jewish prisoners are to remain lined up !". What do they want from us now ?" I thought about the Jewish group from Bidgoshez that disappeared. The answer came soon. We were told to divide ourselves into three groups: POWs from Russia, Polish prisoners from the area under the German military government (between the Bok and the Wisla rivers), and POWs from another area, the largest part of Poland.

Although I was from Mezritch, I stood with the Russia prisoners of war. I did not want to go, or was suspicious of returning home and finding myself under the German occupation that I had encountered while a POW. I preferred the unknown, to go for imprisonment in Russia, assuming those heading for the other locations would be liquidated by the Germans.

Nothing happened for a while. We continued to work as usual. After several more days the Germans began to distribute identity cards to arriving prisoners. If they were distributing official documents to the POWs then maybe they were really being released, I thought to myself. Perhaps it paid to go home ? After considerable thought and self-debate, I mustered the courage to turn to the officer responsible for distributing documents and declared: "I made a mistake in associating with the wrong group, basically my origins are in Mezritch, which is in Poland.", and I immediate waved a letter that I had received from my brother.

The German took the letter, looked at the address, and turned to a map hanging on the wall. He didn't find Mezritch. "There's the city," I pointed from a distance at the map. "You are right." he said when he located the city on the map. "Mezritch is under military rule," he added and thus changed my fate. He ordered an appropriate document for me.

In retrospect I wondered why he had accepted my word without further investigation and didn't ask me why I had registered as a Russian POW. I was surprised.

* * *

"Just imagine the situation I placed myself in by confronting that German officer", Dad said.

* * *

The first transport that left the camp carried Russian Jewish prisoners. Later, when I was at home in Mezritch, I discovered that they were transferred by rail to Lublin. The local Jewish committee refused their plea to stay there. The Yudenrat, who were already strained by the lack of living quarters, could not accommodate the released Jewish POWs of Russian origin; they were transferred to the responsibility of the local SS squad. These SS officers led them by foot through the nearby forests to Biala-Podlaska. On the way their numbers diminished. Some managed to escape and some were killed. The few that managed to arrive at Biala-Podlaska spread across the region, and some of them came to Mezritch as refugees.

The day after the Russian Jewish prisoners had been released we were also called, the group from Biala-Podlaska and Lublin. "You will be released," said the officer in charge. "But do not have any illusion, you are going back home, but not to the home that you left".

We hadn't absorbed the end of the sentence and we started to applaud. For a second we forgot where we were. The German silenced us with shouts.

On March 21, 1940, exactly a year after I had been drafted into the Polish army, we left the POW camp. We were taken by truck to the nearby train station. The group from Mezritch consisted of 12 soldiers, and two German soldiers accompanied us. We passed through many train stations on the way where Polish civilians waited along the way to shower food upon us, convinced that we were Polish soldiers returning home. They didn't consider that we may be Jews. I'm sure that if they had known they would not give us a thing. The German soldiers escorting us didn't know that we were Jews either.

We arrived in Mezritch on Friday night. "You will go directly to the local military headquarters" our escorts barked, "Nobody leaves the convoy!" we were warned. Eidelboim, one of the POWs, convinced the soldiers to let him go home since it was on the way from the train station to their headquarters. They let him go inside for a several minutes and we waited outside. In the short walk to the headquarters he managed to tell us excitedly about his parent's surprise when he entered the house.

The German soldiers took us to one of the public schools in the city, where the headquarters was located.

The rumors of our return spread quickly. When we arrived at the headquarters I was surprised to see my family and the families of several other prisoners waiting there. We felt an enormous excitement in the town. Many people were there, even those we did not know. A little later, other people arrived with big pots filled with food. Actually the German soldiers in our vicinity managed to benefit the most from the abundance of food heaped upon us.

We were registered at the local headquarters, and each one of us was immediately released home. The circle that had begun in September 1939 was closing.

On the way from the train station to the headquarters, and later on the way home, the words spoken by the German prison camp officer before our release echoed in my ears. We would return home, but it would be a different home. His words transformed into reality.

My hometown, Mezritch, "Little America" as it was nicknamed by the residents of neighboring villages, had prospered and flourished in the past, with shop windows filled with merchandise, and on Sabbath Eve exhibited the lively movement of families dressed in their best. This Mezritch became a ghost town. The city was filled with refugees. For the first time in my life I witnessed true scarcity. Total strangers, dressed in worn out and torn clothing, loitered everywhere. Ropes over their shirts replaced belts, and rags substituted shoes. Darkness fell on the city.

The joy of returning home had dissipated with the realization that indeed the city had changed. A different planet, as was said years later by Katzetnik, when describing Auschwitz. My city had become a different planet for me. The happiness of the inhabitants upon our return was genuine but restrained.

I returned from one imprisonment to another kind of prison that I was to meet the following morning.

Sadism or Redemption

March 1940. The sun slowly setting upon a turquoise sky in the outskirts of Lublin did not hint of the coming events. The curfew began at twilight. My only option was to enter the local synagogue and stay throughout the night. The transit permit that I had received from the German authorities was limited to the daylight hours. I didn't know anyone there.

"Where is the closest synagogue?", I asked a local resident. He stared at me a long time. I noticed that he was concentrating on the yellow Star of David on my left arm. It seemed that he suspected something. Nonetheless, he gave directions and disappeared. The instructions were accurate and I quickly found my way to the synagogue.

The large door to the entrance was ajar. The handle and lock were broken. The Mezuzah was missing; instead enormous holes pocked the wooden frame on the upper right side. I still raised my hand in the direction of the missing talisman. I felt an intense burning sensation on my fingers and I put them in my mouth in a kind of kiss, perhaps to soothe the pain.

I went inside. The large empty space was cold. The windows had been smashed. Some of the benches were burned and some were broken. The holy ark was closed. I didn't know what it contained; I assumed that it was empty. Swastikas were sprayed in every corner. I walked slowly to the central stage. The silence was disturbing and the echoes of my steps were clearly audible.

In the far northern corner I saw moving shadows. It must be a candle, I thought. I slowly walked toward the flickering light. I tried to muffle my steps, a habit that I had developed after the occupation.

When I reached the dimly lit room I saw them: three children, two women and four men. They sat on straw. I tried, in the meager light, to estimate their ages. My sudden appearance at the entrance caused them to cower. When they saw my yellow armband they relaxed. One of them signaled that I should sit by his side. When I was seated he turned to me and said in Yiddish that they were from Czechoslovakia. They had come to Poland for a family visit and the war caught them in the village. They couldn't go anywhere. They were surviving on leftover food occasionally supplied by local Jews who were aware of their plight. Since they had entered the synagogue, several months previously, not one prayer ceremony had been conducted. The synagogue was completely deserted.

The spokesman gave me the leftovers of an apple. I bit into it hungrily. Only then did I realize that I hadn't seen food the entire day. My exhaustion from the difficult journey between Mezritch and Lublin on the way to my brother Naphtali, was so great that I fell into a deep sleep immediately.

* * *

The crashing thunderclap of cymbals pierced the night's serenity. He had quietly entered the synagogue, taken two metal pot covers and smashed them together without stopping, while dancing a magical jig. Everyone awoke at once and stared in horror at the shadows of an enormous man who stooped over those sleeping while beating the metal lids against each other. The children began to cry. Their crying and screams mixed with the cymbal's smashing sounds. The noise continued for several minutes that seemed an eternity. Suddenly the cymbal crashing ceased and only the muffled sobbing of the children remained.

The darkness kept me from discovering who he was. One could sense from his heavy breathing that he was apparently a giant of a man.

A match was lit and with it a candle. His profile was illuminated as he placed the candle on the floor. It was terrifying. A white apron-robe covered his clothes. It was clean, and spotless. It glowed in contrast to the surrounding darkness. Everyone stared at the stranger in silence. The giant moved around the room in obvious irritation. He tossed the pot covers in one of the corners and stood with his back towards us.

He suddenly turned around, grabbed one of the men in the room, lifted him like a feather, and dragged him along with him outside the room. The Jew didn't manage to put up any resistance. It all happened in a split second.

Only moments passed and an intense scream was heard coming from the nearby hollow chamber of the synagogue. The scream was so terrifying that some of us covered our ears instinctively and ducked our heads between our shoulders. I had never heard such a wailing. We stared at each other, and no one said a word. The silence that followed the scream was depressing. We crowded into the corners of the room. The children burrowed into their mother's bosoms and disappeared.

I felt that I must do something. I crawled up to the open doorway but didn't see anything. As I tried to rise and leave the room two husky men standing near the doorway blocked my exit and motioned me to return to the corner. Frightened, I crawled back to the corner. A few minutes passed and the giant returned to the doorway. He looked at us and entered. Blood stains could be seen on his white apron. He bent towards the corner of the room and dragged one of the women. She clutched her child in her arms and refused to release him. After a brief struggle the child was thrown to the ground and she was dragged with choking sobs from the room. A few seconds later a terrifying scream was heard, longer than the first, and afterwards another and another. Then they ceased.

Silence.

The child that remained in the room, forcibly separated from his mother, crawled to the woman still there with her two children. She hugged him too.

Someone tried to say something, and a deafening shout was heard from outside commanding absolute silence. And again it was quiet.

The giant returned to the room. More blood stains appeared on his outer-jacket. I found no way to disappear, to vanish into the darkness.

The giant bent over the mother who covered the three chicks with her wings, shook them loose from her, caught the children and squeezed them in his arms. They were screaming, shouting, and crying. He hurried into the hollows of the synagogue and disappeared. All three were in his arms like easy prey and their voices trailed after him like a tail. They refused to be still. But .....

Again silence. And it was yet more depressing.

Suddenly we could hear the terrifying screams of all three children together. And they went on and on, seemingly forever.

The mother remaining in the room began to wail, a wailing ululation that turned into screams that were suddenly stopped by the two husky men who then entered to order silence.

And the giant returned to the room again and again. The spectacle repeated itself: his entry, his bending over, tugging away, leaving, a piercing scream and then silence. The blood stains on his apron, which increased and spread, indicated that something was happening outside; something terrible. I had no doubt that my end was near. There was no way to escape. To fight the two huge men outside with bare hands? Each one was bigger than me, stronger that I was, and obviously armed with something that could easily kill me.

Two of us remained. I was certain to be next, but that's not what happened. I was left alone. My stomach, which was empty, started to grumble. I seemed to pale. I felt absolutely helpless.

Then he entered with a stern look. His apron was totally red with blood. I didn't want to give him the satisfaction of lifting me up, so I arose erect by myself. I stood beside him. He was a head taller than me, a real giant. He didn't say a word, just gazed at me disparagingly, maybe with revulsion, and signaled me to follow him. He went from the room into the synagogue's main hall.

The two large men were not there with our tormentor; just him and me in the holy chamber. For a moment I thought that I had a chance to escape. But the shadows of the husky men in the bashed in doorway of the synagogue disqualified that thought. We slowly walked towards the exit. Our footsteps echoed loudly. We left the synagogue and entered a nearby building. And there, in the open space, all those who had been taken from the synagogue were seated around a metal table; they held slaughtered chickens in their hands and were slowly removing the feathers. The roaring laughter of the three huge men could be heard trailing behind them as they left the building.

A Ray of Light in the Void

The city Mezritch lies on the main road between Poland and Russia, between Warsaw and Brisk. Masses of people passed through there, deciding to escape from Poland to Russia because they thought it would be better during the war. Things happen during war that one cannot comprehend. For example, many families abandoned their children in the city. I didn't search for reasons; we lived with the facts. Almost every day several children without parents were found in the center of town. Lucky ones were taken to a large orphanage that opened in the city. In a brief period more than 100 orphans were gathered there from approximately seventy cities around Poland. As far as I can remember, no children were abandoned by those leaving Mezritch.

The orphanage was managed by Mrs. Mandelblatt, who was assisted by Mrs. Bleiweis. Meager amounts of food and clothing were received by donations. Whoever could contribute, gave. But how much can you give when you have nothing? Obviously, the situation in the orphanage worsened quickly. The number of abandoned children grew and there was no way to accommodate more children there.

One day, towards the end of 1940, the orphanage managers learned that the parents of two children living there were located in Warsaw. And if they are in Warsaw, why shouldn't their children be with them? Thus they decided to return the children to their parents no matter what, and make room for other children. The decision was easy, but its implementation was very complex, since movement from place to place in Poland required special permits that were not easy to receive. My brother Zeev volunteered to accompany the children to Warsaw. That was an exceptional decision.

At this stage Roizke Broit entered the picture; she knew many key people on the German side, and she mediated getting the travel permits for Zeev and the two children towards Warsaw, and for Zeev from Warsaw to Mezritch. The train that left Mezritch for Warsaw suddenly stopped in Shedlitz, and there it was commandeered by the army, which transferred troops from Shedlitz to Warsaw. An army mission took precedence over everything. All the train passengers were expelled and Zeev found himself in a strange town without a grosh (Polish penny), in possession of travel permits that were about to expire, and two children in his care. The strange trio stepped slowly out of the train station, into the unknown.

When will the next train arrive? Can they board it? Where will he find food for the small children and himself?

Walking slowly and hesitantly towards the entry hall of the train station they passed the mail car, the car immediately behind the locomotive.

The German mail clerk who was leaning out of the open window and breathing fresh air turned to Zeev and asked him "Where?"

"To Warsaw", Zeev answered.

The German pointed at the children and asked "Yours?"

"No." Zeev hesitated.

"Who are the children?"

"They were assumed orphans until we learned that their parents are in Warsaw. I volunteered to take them to their parents."

"Enter the car from the other side, you won't be seen from there", said the clerk without hesitation.

It wasn't obvious what motivated the German clerk who was traveling in the mail car of a military transport, once a passenger train, to make Zeev this offer. It was obvious to him that Zeev and the children were Jewish. Astonished, Zeev didn't think twice. Did he have another choice? He collected the two toddlers in his arms and skipped between the locomotive and the mail car to the other side, and with the clerk's help the three of them entered the car that was out of bounds to strangers, especially on this train. If he was caught, the clerk could find himself going East to fight the Russians, or at best to rot in prison or even be executed. Nonetheless he did this deed.

Immediately after the train set out, as the train whistle blew, the German shared his food with them. When they arrived in Warsaw they waited until the last soldier got off. Only after the clerk determined that there was no one in the area, did he instruct them to sneak off carefully, on the other side of the mail car, and get away. They rose onto the platform at a spot where they could mingle with other civilians and so they avoided the need to give the wrong answers to questions they had never been asked before.

Zeev knew Warsaw well and had no trouble finding the address of the parents who suddenly turned into a normal family again. I don't know what the surprised parents spoke about with Zeev and how he answered. Zeev had to return hastily to the train station. His travel permit in Warsaw was about to expire.

Life Under Occupation

I returned to my city of Mezritch following imprisonment by the Germans on March 21, 1940.

The life of the Jews in town from the beginning of the occupation in September 1939 until August 1942 was considered tolerable. Laws and regulations limited our lifestyles but didn't prevent us from living. The experience was less than total freedom but did not reach mass annihilation.

* * *

Before joining the army I received a very warm letter of recommendation from the local electric company manager, in case the management happened to change. The letter described my skills and recommended, if and when I returned to Mezritch, that I be seriously considered for a position with the company. Upon my return from captivity I discovered that the management had changed too much, and therefore I decided to save the letter of recommendation for better times. I settled thus with someone I had worked for in the past – the certified electrician Meir Podolak; even the German Army headquarters that administered the daily life in Mezritch recognized his qualifications. An electrician is sought after in all circumstances, more so a certified electrician. Podolak, who was glad to see me, described my work options. After analyzing the situation we realized that if we could manage to organize a group of professionals we could survive easily and for a long time – a form of mutual insurance. And the results soon materialized. Podolak's group involved three professionals and a coordinator. Meir Podolak, Avram Zuker, and myself were the electricians. The coordinator between us and those seeking our services was Izak Finkelstein, a lawyer who was unemployed since the occupation began and who was very pleased to work with us. Today you would call him a public relations agent. Izak handled all the commercial issues with all those groups seeking professionals like us – electricians.

Who needed electricians during that period? The Germans that controlled the city, including all its departments, were the biggest customers. In the interval from 1940 until the ghetto was built in August of 1942, the German command ordered all kinds of jobs for cash. Attorney Izak Finkelstein, our go-between, found himself working with the German supervisor (from the office that governed the occupied territories). Under orders from his superiors the German would request a job, negotiate the price, and upon its completion would transfer the agreed-upon sum, after approval from his commanders. Luckily, there was no lack of work. The payment was fair and, above all, we were busy every day.

The German also used us as a conduit to accumulate a private fortune. We had not doubt that he presented the authorities with exaggerated receipts and pocketed the difference. If, for example, we requested for a particular job (including materials) 1,000 zloty, he would add a zero to the amount we required. Just a small circle that transformed 1,000 to 10,000 zloty. And who paid attention to small details? The difference went to his private account. The German had no reason to stop working with us. This was a "life cycle" that nobody wished to spoil. I cannot describe life during that period as rosy, but it was life for sure. We, who lived under the German occupation, were also forced to work for them to survive.

Despite the hardship of our circumstances none of us could imagine during this period, that elsewhere there were plans for mass extermination.

* * *

"I have to tell you about Meir Podolak", Dad said one day.

* * *

My friend Meir Podolak was one of the most talented people that I knew. He was self-taught in electricity and electronics. He even established a shop for repairing an assortment of electrical devices. He made his name essentially by repairing radios that would not play.

When Mezritch was occupied by the Russians in September 1939 he and his family fled to Russia to escape the Nazi tyrant that acquired control of the city several days later, as part of the agreement between the two countries.

Podolak, his wife, and his seven-year old daughter traveled to the Ural region, settled in one of the villages and worked there as a technician in the local radio station. A radio in Russia was not like anything we recognized. The radio station was a center broadcasting to a closed network of loud-speakers in the resident's homes and to factories. One could only hear what was broadcast from this station. People did not own any other kind of radio. It was actually forbidden to operate a regular radio. Big Brother decided what and when to broadcast to listener's homes.

After several months, when the family continued to feel out of place in Ural, Meir Podolak decided to return to Mezritch.

German diplomatic representatives in Brisk, where one could register to act on the decision to return to Poland, were the first to tell Podolak and his family to think twice about returning to Mezritch: "The Germans don't love you, you should not return !". This is what they actually said to them.

The couple delegated the final decision to their young daughter. When she was asked where she wanted to go – home to Poland or to remain in Russia, of course the desired answer was obvious – to Poland, home.

The difficulties in Russia and the hope for a better future at home misled some of the escapees, who returned on their tracks and thus sealed their fate.

Mezritch under the German occupation did not wait for the Podolak family. They were forced to live in one room rented from the parents of Sarah Shikersky, a member of my family. The house that they had abandoned several months earlier was already occupied by German soldiers, and it was unthinkable to ask them to leave. The house was abandoned, after all.

* * *

After he settled his wife and daughter into the house, Podolak set out looking for work and quickly found it. The Germans were the only ones looking for craftsmen with Podolak's credentials. Only they could offer work involving electricity and electronics. He got a job at the German army base, in the laboratory that dealt with repairing radio sets and other electrical devices. Radio receivers were limited exclusively to Germans. One of the first sanctions that the German army enforced was to confiscate all the radios belonging to the general population. Within hours all the receivers were collected in the basement of the municipal library and the basement of the local courthouse.

As I said, when I returned from POW captivity to Mezritch I joined up with him and assisted him in his work. One day

I received an order instructing me to travel to Lukov, where we were supposed to fix a broken radio set in the army base cantina. Along with the order we received special permission to travel by train. Without this kind of document we were forbidden from traveling the roads. When we arrived, Podolak inspected the device and found it totally beyond repair.

"It has to be brought to Mezritch", he told the man in charge.

"No problem", was his reply. "Take the receiver and return to Mezritch". But how do you accomplish this? How can two Jews travel on the train with an enormous radio set? The trip in an army transport to the train station was uneventful. At the station we received permission from the local gendarme to lift the device onto a car. The Polish civilians who saw the giant receiver that was banned from their ears fled the passenger car. We figured that if there was an inspection, we could claim that the device was not ours. There had been occasions when people who had tried to smuggle items by train placed them in one car and they themselves traveled in a different car. If the item was discovered, they were safe. If they were not caught, they removed the goods at the journey's end.

The police inspection in the train reached us as well, but luckily the police knew that this was a broken army radio being taken for repair.

We had no problem in Mezritch, and the receiver was transferred with respect by army truck to the laboratory. The repair took several days since we were missing parts, but when it was fixed it was taken to Lukov, this time by soldiers.

Working with the German army gave Podolak and me the opportunity to privately fix electrical appliances belonging to German civilians for a small fee.

Podolak assembled a real radio in his lab from the leftover parts of several broken receivers that we had accumulated. During most of the day it remained disconnected, and in time for the Radio England broadcasts in Polish it was completely pieced together like Lego, becoming our source of information about the situation on the European fronts and other places in the world. With this radio we heard, for example, about the battles at Tobruk. After all you could say that we were fairly well informed. Immediately after the broadcast the receiver was dismantled and became a piece of junk again, among all the other junk lying on the shelves.

* * *

During the *actzias* (military actions to round up Jews) that fell on the city's inhabitants Podolak found refuge in the laboratory. After all, who would search for Jews within an army base? And the army, in general, didn't have a reason to turn people over to the SS. Podolak hid his daughter with a Polish acquaintance for a large sum of money. The latter, after he received the payment, took advantage of the lack of accountability and evicted her from the house. When she couldn't find a hiding place, the girl was killed in Mezritch during the fourth *actzia*.

Podolak's wife was able to hide with a Polish land owner. Podolak arranged a proper monetary contract with him and his wife masqueraded as a Polish woman in every aspect. Of course between *actzias* she worked in his fields.

One day the Polish landlord appeared in the lab and told Podolak that his wife was arrested and taken to Radzin, and for a sum of money he could arrange her release. Podolak didn't ask questions and paid immediately.

A few days later the Polish landlord returned and said: "The money you gave me is not enough, because I need to bribe more people". Podolak tripled the amount of money, and again without argument.

The third time that the story repeated itself Podolak began to suspect foul play. This time, he said to the landlord that before he paid him he wanted to be sure that his wife was still alive. He requested that the man return to Radzin and ask his wife for the date of their wedding anniversary. If he knew then it would be a sign that she was alive.

Several more days passed and the Polish landlord returned and stated, without hesitation, the anniversary date shared by Podolak and his wife. Podolak's face paled. He understood that he had been the victim of a cheat, and worse, that his wife was no longer alive. "Hand over the ring you stole from my wife", Podolak demanded from the surprised Polish man.

"What are you talking about?", he asked Podolak.

"If you don't surrender it, I will tell the soldiers what you are doing", the usually gentle Podolak raised his voice.

"What are you talking about?", the man repeated.

"You hide Jews, pocket their money and then kill them", he said excitedly. "I have nothing to lose. I already lost my daughter, and now I understand that you murdered my wife", he muttered. "Return her ring", he raised his voice.

"I swear that it's not true!" the landlord said, but a low tremble could be heard in his voice.

"Give me the ring!", Podolak shouted. He felt that he was losing his patience. His life was not a life, he didn't care about anything, and this was the only way to regain the last item that belonged to his wife, essentially belonged to him. The Polish man stuffed his hand into his trouser pocket, reached out with the ring for Podolak and disappeared before Podolak could jump on him.

The same Polish landlord did not know the secret pact between Podolak and his wife. They had both agreed, that if and when they were separated and someone asked their wedding anniversary date, it was forbidden to reveal the true date. Each one of them had a wedding ring with the true anniversary engraved within, and only someone who stole the ring or the murderer who stole it would know the actual date.

After the war I met people who survived the war by hiding

with the same Polish landlord. It is likely that the price that they paid, or promised to pay, was so high that this motivated the man to hide them even though the area was declared "Yudenrein", free of Jews.

* * *

Podolak himself survived all the *actzias* by hiding in his laboratory. One of the soldiers, a quartermaster in rank, watched over him and hid him whenever there was a risk. When it became very dangerous, and the soldier feared punishment for being caught harboring a Jew, he told Podolak that he must move elsewhere. This soldier knew a German roadwork contractor living in Mezritch and who worked for a company named "Stauk". The contractor sealed a room in his house on Pilsudskiego Street and Podolak hid there for a period. When the contractor also felt endangered, he told Podolak that he must return to the German quartermaster to care for his cover.

When Podolak felt that he was at the end of his rope, he was smuggled by the soldier onto a train that was on its way to Warsaw. When he understood that he couldn't find a hiding place in the big city, he decided to return to Mezritch. And again, by train, traveling illegally, he returned to Mezritch. Then he suddenly appeared before the German quartermaster and again imposed his safety needs upon him.

The soldier tried the last resort. He took Podolak to the farm area belonging to the Baron Potozky, where a maintenance man named Matishevsky worked and lived.

"Do with me what you want", the desperate Podolak said to Matishevsky.

"I'll see what I can do. But you should know that two of my children belong to the Polish anti-Semitic youth group, and if they know that I'm hiding you, they will expose me – and I will be punished. There is nothing worse than hiding Jews."

Matishevsky led Podolak to his pig pen, and he lived there until the basement that Matishevsky was building under the pen was finished, a secret he shared only with his wife.

For the next two years Podolak kept company with the pigs living above him. He only saw daylight through cracks in the boards. At night he would bring out the pot with his excrement and urine and mixed it in with the pig's muck. The food he received was low quality, and did not come every day. Infrequently he received clean laundry. These were the clothes that his host's wife washed by hand. She was afraid that her maid would suspect her of hiding Jews if she was forced to wash underwear that she did not recognize.

Podolak only came out of the basement when Poland was liberated.[5]

---

5. Meir Podolak returned to Mezritch and concluded that there was nothing for him to seek there. He emigrated to Israel , but after only a few years he moved to Canada with his wife Dora, whom he married in Israel, and with his two children; he lived there for many years until his death. His daughter made Aliyah to Israel several years ago, and his son and wife still live in Canada.

Sochovola

One day in August 1942 the officer in charge of the military unit located in Sochovola (about 40 kilometers from my city) contacted the local commanders in Mezritch and requested 12 skilled workers to make some improvements in their camp. The local German army headquarters contacted the manager of the employment office Mr. Vitola, requesting that he recommend different types of craftsmen. Vitola was a German citizen who employed three local Jewish clerks in his office – the brother of Astusha Bleiweis, the lawyer Izak Finkelstein's brother, and my cousin Chana Rybak – who were also connected to the Jewish community. Vitola and his office clerks knew Podolak's group very well and with their approval recommended me as an electrician. I did not hesitate, I didn't have anything to worry about. I did not fear work.

Vitola developed close relations with the three Jews who worked in his office and even attempted to save their lives. Due to his help two of them survived: Astusha Bleiweis' brother – Astusha was my brother Chaim's girlfriend - and Chana Rybak.[6] Vitola arranged forged Polish identity documents for them with which they managed to pass the entire war in work camps that employed local Polish civilians. Finkelstein's brother was shot during one of the *actzias*, even though he possessed a

---

6. Chana Rybak and Mr. Bleiweis immigrated following the war to Australia and the USA respectively.

Polish identity card. Let's not forget that Polish gentiles were also murdered by the Germans.

Among the group of professionals who gathered in the courtyard of the local military headquarters were two strangers whom I did not recognize – a man and a woman from Warsaw. They were sent by the *Hashomer Hatzair* cell to warn the Jews in Mezritch about an impending *actzia*. We heard about *actzias* but we didn't understand their meaning at the time. The German authorities caught both of them but fortunately they were not killed. The Jewish clerks in Vitola's office, with his approval, took the opportunity afterwards to distance them from the city and certain death.

Before we departed for Sochovola I received an official pass that allowed my travel outside of Mezritch. Documents were critically important in those days and I'll recall this fact later. The document only entitled my stay in Sochovola for ten days.

* * *

The next morning we left for Sochovola, all 12 people, in a wagon harnessed to a single horse. In the early afternoon we arrived at the German army base in Sochovola, which was located on the estate of a Polish nobleman. I don't remember his name, but to the best of my knowledge he was a member of the Polish Cavalry. The nobleman himself managed to escape from Poland as the war began, but his wife remained and was employed by the Germans to do kitchen work and regular chores. The base used to belong to the local cavalry and its central role was training young riding horses before their transfer to the combat units.

We entered the estate grounds and got down from the wagon near the main entrance to the nobleman's palace, where Untersturmfuhrer Shultz awaited us. He commanded us to stand at a certain spot, and by signaling with his stick ordered us to pass him one-by-one for interviews. Each interview was short and transpired while we were standing.

"What's your profession?" Shultz asked.

"A certified electrician", I answered. "And I have an assistant here with me", I added.

"You have an assistant?" he asked, "Who?"

"Him", I said and pointed at the fellow from Warsaw. "He is an assistant electrician." On the way from Mezritch I agreed with the man from Warsaw, who lacked any skills, that he would pose as my assistant.

After my interview Shultz told me and my new friend to stand by his side. He sent the rest of the people to various jobs. As far as I can recall, the woman from Warsaw was assigned to work in the kitchen.

Following all the interviews, Shultz, my new assistant and I made the rounds of the base. Shultz showed us all the places with breaks in the electrical supply that we had to repair. After the inspection tour he brought us into one of the elegant rooms within the palace.

The statement: "It is now 5 o'clock. In another 3 hours, exactly at 8 PM, there's news. I want to hear it!", was shouted at us. Shultz, who stood next to us, had not spoken. I didn't understand who had raised his voice. Sitting in a hidden corner of the same huge room was an officer, apparently of a high rank, who was shouting at us non-stop. It was obvious to both of us what would happen if he didn't hear the news.

We began to work immediately. First of all I looked for the radio's antenna. When I found it on the roof I discovered that the electrical connection had been destroyed, apparently during the occupation of the building; all that was left for me to do was to mend the torn wires. When I discovered what was involved, I stretched a job that should have taken several minutes into several hours, close to the appointed time that I had informed Shultz he should check the radio. The radio worked fine and it received the desired signals.

In one corner of the room an SS officer sat before a piano and played to amuse himself. He ignored us the whole time we were working. When we were done, and sounds from the radio filled the empty space, he called me to appear before him.

"Where are you from?" he asked.

"From Mezritch." I answered.

"And why are you here?"

"To perform professional work according to instructions from the city's headquarters", I said. "We only came for 10 days." I added, and I dug my hand in to take out the work order hidden in my pocket. "Then afterwards we return to Mezritch."

The young officer stared at me disdainfully. He motioned towards me that he was not interested in reading my order.

"Only death will free you from this place." He said, and stretched towards me the leftovers of an apple he had chewed. He apparently knew what was going to happen in the weeks to come.

"What do you want me to do with the leftovers of this apple?" I asked.

The officer motioned his arm towards the trash can that stood about 10 meters away from us. I went to the can and I threw the leftovers inside.

I suppose that the SS officer was sure that I would save the leftovers for myself. For certain, I was hungry and a morsel hadn't reached my lips since the morning and I also didn't know when I would receive nourishment. It appeared natural that apple leftovers would find their way into my hungry stomach. However, I already learned that you never can tell how these sadists will react. The officer could, without difficulty, take the conductor's baton that was lying on the piano and poke it up my nose, or beat me with it, or use it to kill me. Should I give him a reason to become annoyed?" A glance told me that he was surprised that I had not put the chewed-up apple in my pocket.

All the palace rooms were paneled with wood and were all alike. Someone who didn't know the paths through the palace could easily confuse between the rooms. It was like a maze. I was anxious not to open the wrong door and be punished as a result. Fortunately, I found the exit on my first try.

As night fell Shultz transferred us in small wagons to the nearby town of Voyin. The local Jewish police arranged for our sleeping quarters that night.

* * *

The next morning we returned to Sochovola and each person went to their assigned job. Since there were no electrical devices to fix, I was sent to do farm work. My work as a trained electrician was limited to fixing a radio antenna.

In the afternoon Shultz arrived at the field and looked for me. "Brezniak!" he screamed, "Come here!"

I ran to him quickly and walked alongside him in the open field, and what I shall describe now I will not forget until I die.

Both of us, a German and a Jew, were marching side by side towards the palace. Suddenly, without reason, Shultz began to run as if possessed. I didn't understand what was happening, why he was running and where to. I didn't notice anything out of the ordinary. Running in a harvested field was not an everyday occurrence so I looked for the cause of his obsession. In the distance I saw a group of people working, each in their own section, some were hoeing and others were digging. It was typical farm work. I slowly approached them.

I assumed that Shultz had seen that one of the people was momentarily leaning on his hoe and didn't work, and this sight made him crazy. He ran up to the fellow with hysterical strides, pushed him to the ground, and beat him with 25 lashes.

When I arrived nearby he was in the midst of whipping him. He ordered the young man to count the lashes out loud so there wouldn't be any mistakes. From a fair distance I could hear the lashes on skin and afterwards the incrementing count. After 25 blows it was over.

But Shultz still wasn't satisfied and needed something more to calm him down. He shouted in my direction and gestured with his hand that I approach him. It's worth noting that as he began his hysterical sprint I followed his footsteps more slowly. Now this displeased him, to put it mildly.

When I reached him he ordered me to wait and called the Jewish work foreman who was nearby.

"Drop your pants!" he ordered the foreman.

He, who could not believe his eyes and his ears and was terrified, removed his pants and underwear and stood with his lower body totally naked.

Shultz pointed toward a small heap of dust on the ground nearby and ordered the foreman to lie across it so that his behind would be raised a bit. This would make his whipping easier, I naively thought. Indeed, Shultz took the whip, lifted it up in the air, but didn't bring it down. He had another idea.

"Come here!" he screamed at me although I was right next to him.

"Give him 25 lashes!" he commanded.

"I don't whip." I answered quickly.

"Are you disobeying my order?" he roared.

"I don't whip." I repeated my last statement.

"I, a German officer, give an order and you disobey it?" he fumed.

"I am not able to whip." I answered quietly.

Shultz couldn't believe his ears. He began muttering something I could not understand.

"Get up!" he commanded the foreman who had been

witnessing the entire exchange. "You can put on your pants." he said maliciously. For a second it seemed that the episode was over. Then he turned to me and screamed:

"Now you will take off your pants and lie on the mound of dust!" Shultz was very angry and paced about restlessly.

"No one disobeys my orders, and certainly not a Jew."

"25 lashes," he ordered the foreman, "and you count and don't miss any!" he screamed at me.

"One, two, three, ...,ten." When I counted to 10 the whipping ceased.

"Whips I said, not strokes!" Shultz barked at the foreman.

He grabbed the whip from him and whipped me 25 times, and not before he ordered me to count them from the start, one at a time.

When we finished, he with his whipping and I with my counting, I looked back at my behind. It was scarred, bloody, and black in many places. I got up and tied my pants with great difficulty, while Shultz ignored me.

"Drop your pants and lie on the heap!" he suddenly screamed at the startled foreman, and without stopping he turned to me and continued: "And now you shall whip him properly with 25 lashes while he counts. Nobody disobeys my orders." he added.

"I don't whip." I said with my last strength.

"What?" He ordered me to repeat what I said. Apparently he hadn't understood.

"I don't whip." I whispered towards him.

I don't remember the additional 25 whiplashes very well, I'm not certain that I counted them. I just remember that after each one I asked him to kill me. At that moment I preferred to die.

"Are you ready to whip him now?" I heard his voice say after the beating, before I put on my pants.

"I don't whip so kill me." I begged of him.

Shultz refused, but added another 25 lashes to seal the issue.

After 25 lashes and with the subhuman lying before him on the ground, he seemed to relax.

I don't know where I mustered the strength from to get up. I stood up and closed my pants.

"You are coming with me to the palace." he instructed me.

I limped next to him in the direction of the camp. On the way, before we reached the palace Shultz – who had already calmed down – took a sweet- candy from his pocket and offered it to me.

* * *

"Should I have accepted the candy?" Dad asked me, who more than once searched for a moral in his stories. When I hesitated he answered the question himself. "Look, in fact, I'm alive, and apparently what I decided saved my life."

* * *

Should I take the candy? I thought to myself. What would the sadist walking by my side think? If I refused, that would be refusing an order once again. And what would happen if I took it? Indeed a moment ago I asked to die, and now – do I want to live? I don't know what thoughts passed through my mind in those moments. If I took it – would I live? And if I refused – would I die? Suddenly, despite the extreme pain, and despite the crying inside and the tears that welled at the edges of my eyes, I wanted to live. I don't have another explanation for my lifting in spirit at that moment. But I took the candy. "Very nice", Shultz said with satisfaction.

A few days later I saw Shultz whipping a boy who attempted to help a Jewish butcher move a load from one place to the other. This time he didn't use just his whip. He hit him with his fists, his shoes, with stones, and with anything he could lay his hands on. Apparently, administering the whipping brought him to an orgasm, and he only relaxed when he saw the beaten victim lying helpless, but still breathing.

First Actzia in Mezritch

On August 24, 1942, about a month before Rosh Hashana, Shultz called me over and made the following statement: "*Morgen alle Juden kommen raus von Menschenschreck*".

The Germans couldn't pronounce the word "Miedzyrzec" – the Polish name for the city, and called it "Menschenschreck", meaning, people of fear.[7] I never understood who was afraid of whom in the city ....

His statement made my blood freeze. If they were removing the Jews from the city, then where were they taking them? There were rumors but not any evidence. I was afraid and anxious for my family, friends and my acquaintances – and there were many of them. Did they know? Was it possible to inform them? What were they doing and what would they do? Was it possible to save them, and how?

"Because you are from Mezritch", Shultz said, "You will guide me to the Jews' abandoned houses".

To loot. What else? I thought to myself.

"From this moment you do not leave the camp", he ordered.

"I don't think I can help you." I said to Shultz.

"Why?" he asked.

"Because I don't recognize the Jewish section of the city." I lied.

---

7. [Editor's Note: The literal translation of Menschenschreck is public threat]

"In any case you will join me." he ordered.

At night I made a determined effort to leave the camp. I had no lack of excuses and so I managed. On the outside I met a Polish citizen, who took 20 zloty to lead me to the local post office. The German clerk and the Polish clerk in the office were astounded by my request, but a 100 zloty note convinced them to try to locate someone for me in Mezritch. I tried to reach the Judenrat leader, the druggist Klarberg,[8] the dentist Buchenek, and others that I don't recall now. The lines were busy. Even the emergency phone was engaged. I didn't know what to do. I had no way of warning my family so I returned to the camp feeling miserable and desperate.

The next day, August 25 at about 5 AM, I got up onto a military truck. The driver was Polish, Shultz sat next to him, and in the rear section that was covered by a tarpaulin sat myself, my electrician's assistant from Warsaw and two more Jews.

We approached the city from Radzyn. As we got closer to the city, I felt more emotional. Near the Graf (nobleman) Potocki's estate I saw through cracks in the tarp whole families carrying their possessions towards the town center. Among the pedestrians I clearly recognized was the Beer and the Berman families.

Untersturmfuhrer Shultz, who realized that I couldn't assist him in his looting excursion, looked for another local victim. He stopped the truck on Lubelska Street immediately after the bridge that crossed the Krzna (pronounced Kshena) River. Someone told him that in the vicinity of the bridge, on the west bank, lived David Weinberg, a member of the Judenrat who was the middleman between Jews and the army. The distribution of identity documents, travel passes, licenses and such was done through him. Shultz looked for him but he wasn't home.

---

8. Klarberg was the head of the Judenrat in Mezritch and received special privileges from the Germans. His image is controversial among the city's Jews.

Untersturmfuhrer Shultz directed the truck driver to the house of Klarberg the druggist.

The trip from the river to the center of town usually took only a few minutes, but due to the crowds flowing toward the center and the presence of hundreds of soldiers, police and SS, we were forced to move very slowly. The closer we got to the square, the clearer the dreadful picture became. To start with I heard the dogs barking and then the soldier's shouts and the sound of shots that echoed from all directions. I was filled with anxiety. I moved about restlessly in the rear of the truck from crack to slit trying to see what was happening. I couldn't believe my eyes.

The truck halted next to the city hall, which was near the druggist Klarberg's house. Klarberg was outside staring at the commotion. Shultz, who ignored what was happening around him, ordered him to point out someone who could lead him to the houses abandoned by the Jews. Klarberg implicated the Jewish assistant to the Polish tax collector Sloviansky, who knew the location of all the Jewish homes.

While we were waiting for the assistant to arrive, I stared at the scene and listened to the deafening sounds. I saw many sitting on the ground and waiting. Whoever stood up – was shot. Within the throng I saw activists who attempted various schemes to extract their family members from the square. From the unknown back to life. Several indeed managed to get out, but many others refused because they didn't want to abandon their families.

The brother of Shprinze Zemel, for example, didn't want to leave his son, and Mr. Wiener, who had permission to leave the square, remained with his wife who had not been released. Later on I was told that when it became apparent to the commander of this *actzia* that the group he had assembled was shrinking, he abruptly raised his arms and shouted: "no more releases".

I saw Berka Finkelstein standing next to the truck; he was

the brother of Regina (today Grinboim). Berka's job was to collect metals and raw steel. He was waiting for the German who employed him to arrive with his horse and wagon. He wore a large sign on his chest that clearly displayed his special status. Berka leaned on the truck complacently and chewed a juicy apple. I went to the opening in the rear and told him that he should jump into the truck and escape by bribing Shultz. Berka grinned. He was certain that his German would come soon and take him to work. Like many others, Berka died on the train before reaching Treblinka.

In contrast, Roizika Broit saved the ring on her finger and managed to buy a few more days of grace. She joined us in the truck after her ring became Shultz's property.

When the tax collector's assistant arrived, the truck started moving in the direction of Pilsudski Street. There were many of our people's dead bodies along the way and in the truck's path. There were those among the Jews who only hours earlier had fled to Polish families while carrying their bundled treasure, in the hope that this would save them. But these so-called Polish friends killed the Jews themselves and tossed their bodies into the street. The Poles robbed and killed the Jews that were on their way to the city's central square. These local Poles had beaten Shultz to his plunder.

The dead bodies strewn along the way caused the truck driver to occasionally mount the sidewalk and travel quite slowly, even slowing to a crawl.

The assistant instructed us to go from house to house. To his dismay, Untersturmfuhrer Shultz did not find anything of immediate value in these houses. Only clothing remained. This had value, since Shultz knew that he could easily sell clothing in the vicinity of the camp.

I recall that one of the houses that Shultz entered had belonged to Chaim Weingerik. Dr. Gad Lichtenberg lived in one of his apartments. It appeared that they had left only a few moments before we arrived. There were bundles of clothing assembled in the house, each tied with rope, and this made Untersturmfuhrer Shultz's looting task much easier. As a result Shultz filled half the truck with clothing and ordered the Polish driver to return to the base.

It was 4 o'clock in the afternoon. We traveled on Warshawska Street and turned onto Lubelska Street, once the main promenade for traditional Sabbath afternoon strolls before the war. We only managed to reach the corner of Koshalna Street and Lubelska, in the central square, and stopped. While standing in the rear of the enclosed truck, I moved the tarp slightly and saw many of my acquaintances, friends and family for what was to be the last time. All of them were marching to the train station. A convoy of families, both adults and children slowly moved towards the unknown. The surrounding Germans escorted them with screams and shots mixed with the barking of dogs. A long convoy that was seemingly endless. Even on the way to the train station from the central square one could witness the terrible treatment of the Jews by the Germans. A herd of cattle would get more consideration. Anyone straying from this path was executed immediately.

The convoy of Jews crossed the Krzna River on Lubelska Street and turned left onto Zarovia Street (now called The Partisan's Street) in the direction of the train station. We waited in the truck until the convoy had passed, and when a path was cleared we returned in the direction of Sochovola. We parted ways with Roizika Broit in the town of Radzin; she perished later too.

It is hard to describe my feelings. The transformation that a person undergoes when watching these kinds of images is terrifying. Your memory becomes dysfunctional, and names that you pronounce aloud suddenly disappear as if they never existed. I felt that my whole body was withering and evaporating. The only thing echoing in my head was that 400 years of beautiful Jewish culture were disintegrating. The foundation and character of this culture were vanishing before my eyes.

* * *

The following day, the second day of the *actzia*, I decided to slip away from Shultz's looting trip. I wanted to know what had happened to my family. When Shultz found a new guide, a policeman by the name of Brokash whose father was chief of police, and I saw that he was busy looting, I got away. I quickly arrived at my parent's house. The house had been broken into. I went up the staircase and didn't find anybody. From the anxiety I began to shout, rather to scream, the names of my family members. After a while that seemed like an eternity someone answered me from the attic. And then they described for me what happened to them yesterday, the first day of the *actzia*.

My family had decided to ignore the Germans' announcements and they didn't leave for the square. They were not the only ones. Many of them understood the meaning of going out towards the square. At that time a tailor and his family lived in our parent's house, refugees from the village of Nasielsk who moved to Mezritch after the beginning of the war. Opposite their house was a building belonging to a vocational school that was being guarded by a Polish watchman.

A few days before the *actzia* the guard had ordered a pair of pants to be made by the tailor, who had promised to complete them on exactly the day that the *actzia* began. When he realized that these pants would not reach him, he decided to enter my family's house and take them himself. But that same morning the Germans had posted decrees all over the city stating that whoever entered a Jew's house – would be shot. As a result the guard was faced with a serious dilemma – his pants or his life. If he entered alone he would certainly be shot. Therefore he appealed to a group of Ukrainians who were gathered nearby the house and asked one of them to join him for protection. The Ukrainian refused since at that moment he was busy operating a phonograph he had looted from an abandoned house, to play a record for his friends. And what was the wonderful song that kept the Ukrainian from accompanying the Polish guard? A cantor's rendition of Kol Nidre, our most sacred prayer! In desperation, the guard turned to one of the military police who was stationed in the area. The German policeman, who understood that saving lives was involved, accompanied the Polish guard and they both entered the house. Suddenly they encountered my entire family on the top floor.

The German policeman stared at my family, which he recognized. Instead of exposing them, he ordered them: "Do what you have to, but you must disappear from here!" He didn't care how they vanished, just that they were gone. The policeman turned to the guard who was clutching his new pants in his hands and threatened him, that if, God forbid, he should leak what he had seen and heard there – he would be shot.

After a brief deliberation the family decided to go up to the attic and remain there until the upheaval outside passed.

On the evening of the same day, after the train carrying Jews left for an unknown destination, the same German military policeman appeared at my family's home with a horse and wagon, gathered all the youngsters from the attic and transported them across the river – to the dwellings of Jewish families who worked for the German army. Thus they were saved from this *actzia*. The adults who remained stayed in the attic.

After the short visit at my family's house I searched for the tracks made by the truck in order to return to Sochovola.

On the way, on Warshawska Street, I noticed that someone was following me. I tried to lose him, but to no avail. One of the locals recognized me and didn't let me go. "He is a Jew." the Polish local said to Shultz.

Shultz turned to him and acted as if he didn't understand.

"He should be in the city square." added the other.

And what did Shultz do? He drew his pistol and chased the parasite away with his screams.

The third day of the *actzia* was devoted to gathering the bodies of the dead and to cleansing the city of the terrible events that had affected it and its Jewish occupants. When the *actzia* was over the Jews were evicted from their homes and they went to live in the ghetto.

* * *

Several days after the *actzia*, I decided to escape from the base in Sochovola. Actually, I could have escaped from Voyin where we spent the nights, but I did not want the Jewish police, who were responsible for us, to be punished as a result. It was not difficult to escape from Sochovola, either. The base was open, compared to other places that I had encountered in the past. I was concerned about what would happen in Mezritch because of my escape. I feared that the Germans, and especially Shultz, would search for me.

Despite my concerns, I organized the escape with the boy who helped the Jewish butcher. We were both blue from the lashings we had endured. On the day of our escape each of us wore two pairs of pants. We knew that you could receive a half a loaf of bread for a pair of pants on the outside. We passed through the forests and fields that surrounded the main roads between Sochovola and Mezritch. Bartering the pants into bread was not easy. A Polish peasant farmer refused to give us bread, until he felt threatened. Then he gave us a half a loaf. We arrived at Mezritch that night.

I returned to the city for the second time. The city was unrecognizable to me. This time all the Jews who remained after the *actzia* were crowded into the ghetto. My house was not within the ghetto boundaries so my family went to live with my uncle Baruch Lynn, the municipal slaughterer, part of whose family was taken to Treblinka[9] during the first *actzia*.

---

9. Both of the translator's grandparents, Joseph and Esther Tchemny were forced onto that train to Treblinka, where they perished.

The Tshenky Brothers

On the 28th August 1942, immediately following the *actzia*, the Jewish ghetto was established. The area was surrounded by a barbed wire fence, and Jews from the town and those deported from other regions were concentrated in the ghetto. Fortunately for my family, Uncle Baruch Lynn's house was within this ghetto, so I could move there with my brother Zeev, the Shainberg Family and with the tailor's family that had been deported from Nasielsk.

At the time of the first *actzia*, and perhaps afterwards, we had no idea where they took all those who had been caught. Thousands of zloty were paid to Polish families to investigate where the trains went to, but without results. The Germans managed to eliminate information about the train tracks, and we didn't know where they had taken our loved ones.

A few days after the *actzia* the two Tshenky brothers appeared in the ghetto, having been on the transport leaving town during that *actzia*. They told us that they escaped from the death camp Treblinka by overcoming impossible obstacles: after the fateful life-or-death sorting they were assigned to remove bodies from the arriving transport trains, and afterwards – to load clothing onto the same cars. During one of the loadings they remained inside the car and hid inside heaps of clothing. And that is how they escaped.

When they arrived in Mezritch they ran to expose the German Reich's biggest secret that had fallen into their hands – "The Final Solution". They rushed to explain that Treblinka was neither a vacation spa nor a work camp. Treblinka was a camp of destruction, a death camp. They chose to disclose these facts to Shalom Weinberg who was one of the Judenrat officers. The brothers were anxious to warn those responsible for the community not to assist the Germans in rounding up Jews, since they were not leaving for work but to an extermination camp.

Shalom Weinberg did not believe them and even tried to deny the story and said that they didn't know what they were talking about. And in order to prove that they are wrong he said he would clarify these facts with Heine, the SS officer from Radzin. Two hours after the information was passed to Heine the two Tshenky brothers were already dead. Shalom Weinberg, who had told the surprised German about what was apparently happening in Treblinka, was ordered to bring the two brothers to him so they could tell him the lie from their own lips. The meeting point did not reveal their fate. They were not ordered to the headquarters, but rather to the pharmacy owned by Klarberg who was head of the Judenrat. Their naivety was their downfall. Both of them arrived wanting to tell the truth even to the German officer. As a prize they were invited to join him for a short trip in town. When they crossed the main square and arrived at the arches on the other side, the German officer drew his pistol in one of the alleys and killed both brothers with only two shots. It goes without saying that he sent Shalom Weinberg to take care of removing the bodies.

From that moment on there was a significant shift in the behavior of the Jews. It was obvious to everyone that death would ambush us at the final station of those trains leaving Mezritch.

Three Events

Among the Jews there were those who collaborated, or those who we thought were collaborating with the Nazis. Everybody wanted to live, and life was apparently priceless.

Chaim Rogozin, who was Roizke Broit's husband, escaped to Russia when the war began, while it was still possible. Life in Russia apparently was not good for him and he decided to infiltrate back into Poland. The Germans tightened their defenses particularly along the Russian border, making it almost impossible to cross between the countries. Unfortunately for Rogozin, he was caught by the Gestapo and arrested. The news of his arrest reached his wife. She made every effort to free him but met sealed walls.

The rumor spread that only after negotiations with many connected people was she told that if she agreed to divulge information to the Germans, meaning to collaborate, her husband would be freed. And then, several days later, Rogozin was freed. I don't know the price that was paid to the Germans for his release, but Roizke Broit was marked with an indelible stain.

* * *

When the Germans wanted a certain job done, they approached the Judenrat, or another Jewish institution, and demanded a

Jewish quota for work. They gave two parameters: the number of workers required and the duration. The quota had to be filled at the appointed time. The Judenrat began searching for Jews and collecting them from the courtyards in town. Waves of rumors passed across the city that they were looking for Jews, and whoever was caught looked for a way to escape.

How was that done? Connections and bribery. And this despite the fact that the quota had be filled and someone else, perhaps a family member or close friend, would replace the person who was freed. Connections, money, diamonds, gold or other expensive equipment worked well as an offering for release from the unknown.

One of the possible "scams" was to convey to the Judenrat the names of wealthy people, above the required quota and just before these names were delivered to the Germans for release, to indebt them for their freedom. These pardons from the labor squads were intolerable to us.

"Your lives were spared because of Roizke Broit's intervention", was claimed more than once by the Germans who released those people with means.

And when they met her afterwards she apologized for their being rich enough and they could pay for their lives.

Did Roizke Broit pass the names of wealthy Jews to the Germans in order to release them, and thus create an obligation to her? Did she profit from this trick? I don't have the answer.

* * *

The rumor spread around town that Roizke Broit convinced a youth by the name of Z' to work with the Germans. The process of persuasion was similar to what she had endured to release her husband, Chaim, in return for collaboration. The same fellow Z' had a girlfriend in Brisklibsk, a small town in Russia. When war erupted Z' escaped to join his girlfriend.

As time passed and he returned to Mezritch he was caught, arrested and charged with spying. Roizke Broit convinced him that his life was more important. He understood, was released and began spying and essentially – informing.

For a time after his release from jail Z' started dating Astusha Bleiweiss, formerly the girlfriend of my brother Chaim who went to Australia. At this stage she still maintained contact with my brother. Zeev and I suspected that Z', in order to destroy evidence that he was seeing Chaim's girlfriend, would inform on us to the Germans. Things like this happened more than once.

A few months later Astusha dumped him in favor of Boidman, the post office manager in the ghetto; he was in the underground and a short time later they decided to marry. A day before the wedding Boidman was taken to be killed. Someone arranged that the list of underground members seeking false identification papers would reach the Germans. Boidman's name was among them.

Was this a case of intentional informing?

Astusha was shot during one of the *actzias* as she tried to escape the convoy that was traveling towards the train.

Roizke Broit was killed by the Gestapo in the main town square during the fifth *actzia*.

The Pistol

The sound of the blaring siren bothered me. What was happening? Another exercise by the army, military police, or the Gestapo? I continued in my attempt to repair an electric oven with a burned out heating element.

"Fire", the German master-sergeant exclaimed with excitement. He entered the room from the far side and stormed across. He saw that I was working there, gestured something with his hands, and disappeared out the second door on the other side. Only his voice was heard from a distance: "fire, fire".

I never thought that it was a fire. This was the first time that I heard a real emergency alarm in the camp where I worked. Let them burn, I thought innocently. But what about me? I didn't have to answer. The master-sergeant returned to the room and was surprised that I hadn't reacted to his call. He scolded me and ordered me to go out to the yard at once and to help extinguish the flames.

There was a big commotion in the yard. Flames were engulfing the camp's arms-store. The soldiers and German police gave orders to all who were there, Poles and Jews. Everyone labored to put out the fire and I joined too. Buckets of water were mostly used. There was a risk that the flames would ignite the explosives in the neighboring warehouse, therefore the Germans sent us to extinguish it. They knew that only if we were in danger would we help them. Indeed, a short while later the fire was out.

The German soldiers could celebrate another victory. I am certain that they drank themselves drunk that night, like the previous nights, but this time there was a reason to celebrate.

* * *

"I stole a pistol." I heard my friend Zvi-Hirsch Zilbergleit whisper two days after the fire. "While fighting the fire I noticed a pistol rolling on the warehouse floor and I took it" he added, simply.

"Why are you telling me this?" I asked.

"You were in the army and you can teach me how to shoot it." he replied.

"Do you have bullets? I asked.

"No."

"And where is the pistol?" I asked him.

"I hid it in a bucket and buried that in the ground not far from my house". Zvi-Hirsch pointed out the exact location of the pistol.

"Let's see what the day brings", I said without elaborating.

Now we had a pistol. We, I emphasize, since I had become a partner because of the secret. Frankly I didn't know what to do. I didn't have any connections with the underground or the partisans. We had heard about them but I didn't have any substantial information. Inside the ghetto there was no organized resistance against the Germans. On the other hand, the number of informants was ever-increasing. People were prepared to inform on their family for a parcel of food. The Germans did not check if the information was correct. They beat or shot the informant's victim. Everyone worried only about themselves.

And suddenly I find myself "partner" to weapons smuggling.

Truthfully, this thing was not to my liking, to say the least. It is true that Zvi-Hirsch was my friend. But since his parents died in the *actzia* his behavior had changed drastically. Guilt feelings over their death weighed heavily upon him. He drank to distraction to relieve his emotional pain, and more than once I found him intoxicated. Zvi-Hirsch was ready to do anything to secure another drop of alcohol. I was afraid to fall victim to his divulging information foolishly.

Did he bind me to him? I thought to myself. And what was I to do? I was concerned that one day he would say: "Moshe Brezniak also knew". A day passed and them another and I avoided bringing up the subject. At night I would ponder a solution to the strange situation I was drawn into against my will.

The pressure of events and the daily suffering removed the pistol from my daily agenda. Until today my body gets the chills when I recall the story about the pistol.

The Expulsion
from Mezritch

The sixth of October 1942 began like any other day. A bad day, but nothing that indicated what was to come.

"An *actzia*" was the anxious shout heard from my relative, Baruch Mordecai Reinwein who was Naphtali's son. "The Germans have opened fire and they are rounding up Jews again". It was the afternoon, and as stated there was no indication in town beforehand. So suddenly, in midday, an *actzia* fell upon us from the sky.

I literally flew with Baruch to the basement of the building we worked in. We ran down the stairs extremely fast, as if a fireball was chasing after us. When we reach the basement we entered one of the closets, locked ourselves in from within and hid. A few minutes later we heard voices in German. Someone was looking for us, but made no great effort. He apparently skipped searching in the basement and went back upstairs.

After the last *actzia*, we had prepared the basement hiding place exactly for these circumstances. Several times I even practiced a quick descent to the basement and entry into the same large closet that had sacks of potatoes within.

"It's worth preparing for the worst and seeking a hiding place." I remember telling everyone who worked with me. "Difficult during training and easy in battle." I quoted my officer in the army as saying.

"This time they missed us." I said to Baruch afterwards.

At night, when we thought the commotion had passed and the place was quiet, we left the closet hiding place and returned to our work area.

Another dangerous wave had passed.

The nights and days after the second *actzia* I spent in the camp. I was afraid to return home. Fortunately, rounding up the Jews who worked in the military camp was limited to the initial hours of that *actzia*, which lasted for three days. The Gestapo soldiers dragged to the main square those Jews who they caught in other parts of town.

In that *actzia* my aunts Rachel Rybak and Perl Lynn were shot dead, as they tried to escape the round-up. Whoever remained was sent to Treblinka.

* * *

During this period I worked as an electrician in the camp headquarters situated across the river, on the left side of the road to Lublin, and I was given the appropriate papers. I possessed another document that declared that I also worked in the pig-bristles factory that was in Kur de Lar, on the other side of the army base.[10] Although Mezritch was a world center for pig-bristles processing, I had never worked in this field, but I managed to obtain the proper document. Papers were very important; they enabled existence outside the ghetto. With their help one could move from place to place, with trepidation, but less worry.

---

10. In October 1940 a representative of the German Commerce Ministry arrived in Mezritch to nationalize the factories that processed pig-bristles and manufactured brushes. Many of these factories were owned by Jews. All of the factories were grouped under a single management and scores of Jews worked under tough conditions.

* * *

The third *actzia* started on the October 27, 1942. On that day I was repairing an electrical short circuit in the bristles factory in Kur de Lar. Breakdowns in the electrical system were quite common during that period. Luckily, I told myself, the storm passed on the other side of the army camp. Real luck. This time they rounded up the Jews in the camp and they also found those that hid in the basement closet that contained sacks of potatoes, where I had hidden during the previous *actzia*. Apparently, according to an order from above, the Gestapo was not allowed into the factory on that day, and so I was spared. The next day, when the Gestapo was allowed to enter the factory to search for Jews, I was present in the army camp across the street. I didn't hide because this time they skipped the camp.

What could I derive from these two terrible days? Is there someone who directs the fate of a person, this time my fate? Only my being in the right place at the right time had saved my life. In both instances the eye of the storm had passed within 50 meters of me.

* * *

In contrast to the Gestapo, the military police remained in the city for a long period. Some of them even established relations with several Jews and protected them from the Gestapo during the *actzias*. During the third *actzia*, for example, the military policed assembled about 30 Jews. One of the military police officers told the Gestapo who tried to pounce on these Jews that it was an essential group which had been specially chosen to perform a special task for the military police. In fact, the people in the group received digging hoes before being sent into the forest to dig up roots. When the rage of the *actzia* passed this group of Jews returned to the army camp, gave back their hoes and were released. My brother Zeev, who told me about it, was among the survivors. As far as I know, the military police did not fire upon the Jews.

This *actzia* ended in Treblinka, exactly as the previous *actzias* had.

* * *

The fourth *actzia* occurred on the 7th and 8th of November 1942.[11] It was an *actzia* of surrender. No one in the ghetto had the strength to resist the Germans any more. Many surrendered of their own will. So great was the hunger and so terrible was the desperation, that death seemed like an excellent solution.

I still worked as an electrician and the future still appeared too gloomy.

---

11. When word spread that many Jews were hiding in bunkers that they had built, the Germans renewed their search. On the 7th of November a special search unit was brought to Mezritch that was assisted by dogs. Those caught were sent to Treblinka.

Shleiger

"There's no switch available." I told the master-sergeant who was responsible for the laboratory.

"You looked in the warehouse?" he asked.

"There haven't been any switches for several days." I answered.

The master-sergeant disappeared. "You are going out to the city to buy switches." he said when he returned a few minutes later.

Electrical goods could only be purchased at the appliance store that was owned by Shuma Rosenblum. The store owners had changed – all the shops belonging to Jews were turned over to Poles. The shop district was off-limits to Jews. The city center was totally forbidden.

"I'm not permitted to be there." I said.

"I forgot." the master-sergeant said and he left the room again.

He returned several minutes later. "I'm going out with you." he said. What could happen to me if I go with a German soldier, I thought to myself.

As we left the camp I noticed that the master-sergeant was without a weapon. "Maybe you should take a gun." I told him.

"Do you intend to escape?" he wondered.

"It is better if you are armed." I pointed out.

"Why?" he asked innocently.

He is just dumb, I said to myself.

"What will the Gestapo, who are all over town, say if they see an unarmed soldier walking around with a Jew?" I asked of him.

"You are right." he answered. We returned to camp and went out again only after he had equipped himself with a gun. Even though I was accompanied by a German soldier I had to be sure that I had all my documents and that the Star of David band was fastened on my arm.

The electrical appliance store was on Lubelska Street, between the city square and my family's house, situated on the corner of Warshawska Street. Going to the store and purchasing the switch was straightforward. It was sad to see what had happened to the city in the months that passed since the first *actzia*. There was no resemblance to the bustling life that characterized it in the past. Here and there a few Poles circulated in the square with nothing to do.

"Here was our family store", I pointed out to the master-sergeant as we passed it on our way back near the square. But this fact didn't interest him very much.

Just before the bridge over the Krzna River I was stunned. I stopped breathing. I was confronted by Franz Bauer the terrible – Shleiger – whose name induces in me, and I am sure in others, shivers and tremors until today.[12] He was known for his need, his compulsive need, to kill someone every day in order to satisfy his physical urges. Shleiger did not need a reason to kill. Before he executed the sentence he would roar at his victim, "Why are you running?, Why are you standing?, Why are you sitting?", and kill him without blinking an eyelid. There was a shout, followed by a shot. It was always in the back of the neck or head. And he was done. Sometimes he did not scream, but

---

12. Franz Bauer was a junior Gestapo officer who excelled in his barbarity. He used to walk through the alleys of the ghetto accompanied by dogs that snarled and pounced upon whoever they passed, especially children.

ask the question pleasantly, and then fired a shot. He did not wait for an answer.

The sight before me was not encouraging. Quite the opposite was true. I saw that Shleiger had dragged a small child to the yard and immediately heard an indistinct shout and one shot. Although I was close by, I did not hear the child. A disturbing silence accompanied the shot.

"Shleiger killed another child", I said to the master-sergeant. He didn't respond. It seemed to me that the incident had not impressed him. We did not stop even for a moment. We passed the yard and advanced back to the camp. We did not deviate from our path.

"Come to me", Shleiger called as he left the yard and he saw us leaving. We turned. Standing a short distance from me was the chief butcher of the town. I was certain that my bitter end had come.

"This Jew is essential", the master-sergeant told Shleiger.

"Who is he that he is so essential?"

"He works for the army".

"So what?" Shleiger said nonchalantly, as if he had not slain a child with his own hand a few moments earlier.

"He is essential and we need him", the master-sergeant answered.

"I'm in charge here", Shleiger said, as my special qualifications really did not interest him.

I felt the blood drain from my body. I became petrified. The child was the appetizer of the day and, apparently, I was the main course.

Shleiger stepped up and came between myself and the master-sergeant. I looked at the pistol fastened to his belt. "You know that you are forbidden to walk in the street?" he screamed at me.

Now comes the shot. The show must follow the script. A screaming question and then the shot. I waited a moment and nothing happened. Shleiger did not shoot. For a moment the thought crossed my mind to jump on him and display the last resistance. I don't remember what exactly kept me from doing this. Shleiger raised his head upwards for a second, lowered it slowly and said without waiting for my answer: "Go to the Jewish police and tell them to send someone to collect the child's body". Then he turned, called to his friend from the Shutzpolice who stood nearby, and walked slowly to the city square.

Like with every anxiety-provoking experience, my accelerated heartbeat was felt in my chest, my ears and my head for some time afterwards. My pulse continued to race for much longer than usual.

Later on I was told that my cousin Rivka Sheinberg and her mother, who was in the opposite building and peeked through the shutters, had seen the incident: the murder of the child and the exchange regarding me with Shleiger (the building belonged to David Weinberg). They both knew Shleiger very well, his abuse and the stories about him and they were certain that my end had come.

You can hear the stories about Shleiger the murderer and his awful, abusive acts from any remaining survivors who were in Mezritch and its surroundings.

Willful Deportation
to Trevniki

On the 26th of December 1942, after the fourth *actzia*, the Germans announced that whoever wanted to travel to the hair-brush bristle factory in Trevniki could do so. Although this was "deportation by consent", or "exile by choice", I decided not to go. Even though the future in Trevniki seemed better than the future in the ghetto, I did not believe a word the Germans said. There is no good without bad, this I had learned. Even the fact that my father had lived in Trevniki did not encourage me to leave Mezritch, where I felt closer to my family, especially my brother, and more secure since I knew all the secret paths so well. So even though the Germans did not actively seek "volunteers", I remained scarce while the train to Trevniki was still waiting.

One of the German soldiers who knew me from his extended stay in town, and who had been responsible for my work several times in the camp, hid me inside the army's food warehouse. He also realized that "exile by choice" didn't promise anything. This soldier told the kitchen manager that Avraham Zucker and I were hidden in the basement, in the storage room, and requested that he not let the Polish workers, who may inform on us, enter until the train to Trevniki left. Towards the end of December the German told us that he was taking leave but we should not be concerned. He provided us with food for several days. "No one will enter the storage room because they have nothing to look for here", he added. After several days he returned and released us from the storage room.

And how do you thank a German soldier who probably saved your life? Yes, these things also happened in this horror. Both of us, Zucker and I, bought a gift for the German officer – riding pants and gloves. The German refused to accept the gift. Only after our persistence did he accept the gift, on condition that we would accept a gift from him in return – blankets and a bottle of strong spirits that he himself had received for the holidays.

But how do you bring blankets and strong drink into the ghetto? How do you smuggle something into the ghetto with gates that were sealed shut and tightly monitored so that nothing entered? Whoever was caught smuggling food or equipment – was punished. Often they were shot on the spot. One of the more successful methods was to toss the goods over the fence, hoping that someone from your family was on the other side to catch what you threw. Sometimes you succeeded in throwing the package over but it would disappear, because a foreign hand had caught it. And who ever found it – took it.

This time I took the blanket, wrapped it around my stomach and wore my clothes and coat over it. And it's worth remembering that in January it's very cold in Poland. That evening, I anxiously stepped through the gate into the ghetto along with other Jews who were returning from work.

"Stop!" yelled the German at the gate.

I continued to walk. In my innocence I thought that he had meant someone else.

"Stop!" the shout was heard again.

"Me?" I turned and pointed at myself.

"You!" answered the German and motioned for me to approach him. I trembled so much that my legs almost failed but I did not fall. I walked towards him slowly. "Go over there!", he ordered me and pointed to another soldier standing in our vicinity. I approached the soldier who appeared bored and was not paying attention to what happened.

The soldier who had given us the blankets probably informed on us, I thought to myself, but I immediately rejected that thought. He actually saved our lives a few days ago and it wasn't likely that he would have exposed us.

"Open the coat", he said with great indifference. It appeared as if I was disturbing his rest.

Slowly I opened the coat that covered the shirt I was wearing that covered the blanket. "Close the coat", he said with the same indifference, even though I hadn't finished opening it. Is he drunk? I asked myself. "Go away!" he added and the color returned to my face. Zucker, unlike me, gave up trying. He left the blanket in the storage room.

I gave the blanket that I had smuggled into the ghetto to the tailor from Nasielsk who still lived in my uncle's house, and the pants that he created from the material was then sold so my family could survive several more days.

When I returned to the ghetto I discovered that about 500 Jews went willingly onto the train that left for Trevniki on December 30. Nobody was forced. My family who lived in the ghetto refused to travel to Trevniki. Each one of them found another method to avoid the area. During the period of their absence their houses were broken into and everything that could be taken, such as clothing and cooking utensils, was stolen. The number of Jews remaining in the ghetto was dwindling.

Years later I found out that everyone who had allowed themselves be deported to Trevniki was taken to the brush-bristle factory that was set up in Maidanek; they were killed during the "harvest festival", as the infamous day was called when thousands of Jews were massacred on a hill overlooking Lublin.

Murder in the Ghetto

One day before the fifth *actzia*, Shimon, a Jewish policeman, was found dead. The cause of death was obvious – Shimon was shot in the head at short range. Death and corpses were part of life in the ghetto. There wasn't a day when we did not see bodies rolling in the street. But a dead policeman's body that was shot and not emaciated from hunger or from disease was considered a big surprise even then. And who would want to kill Shimon? We had a hunch that Scholeize the policeman was the murderer.

Even though the authorities didn't consider human life worth anything, the murder of a Jew by another Jew was a serious crime. It was mandated to investigate the event and find the killer.

The investigation was conducted by Scholeize. Ironically he, the main suspect, at least in the opinion of us Jews, led the investigations.

At first Shimon's girlfriend was arrested and interrogated for several hours. Eli, Shimon's brother, who suspected that Scholeize was the one who killed Shimon, told his brother's girlfriend before her arrest not to disclose whom they suspected.

"I saw the murderer's shadow", the girlfriend stated at her interrogation. "And the shadow was very similar to yours", the girl added when she was requested to describe what she saw.

"Are you saying that I killed Shimon?", Scholeize asked.

"I am telling you that the murderer's shadow resembled you", she replied.

How do I know about everything that occurred in the interrogation room? Know the text? My friend Finkelstein's brother, who was also a policeman, leaked to us what went on in the inner chambers of the Jewish police.

At the end of the interrogation the girlfriend was released. No one was arrested. No one was charged with Shimon's murder.

And why was Scholeize suspected of eliminating Shimon? Some time before Shimon's murder Plata Stein died, and he had some kind of money dispute with Shimon. Plata's untimely death was investigated, but no one was suspected of causing his death. Everyone assumed that he died of natural causes. Scholeize, a very close friend of Plata's, suspected Shimon and even told this to his friends. One day he decided to act on his suspicions. He was a judge without a trial as well as the executioner. One day, when Scholeize and Shimon – both policemen on duty – were walking between the houses of the ghetto, Scholeize apparently drew out his pistol and shot Shimon. In any case, two investigations yielded no evidence.

Plata Stein died between the *actzias* and was buried in the Jewish cemetery. On his tombstone was inscribed: "Here lies Plata Stein, who was killed during the German occupation". Just like that: during the German occupation. As far as I know, that is the only tombstone that was inscribed this way.

* * *

"In the course of time", Dad said to me," the story of Shimon's murder grew wings. First the myth of the Jewish underground was established, which as far as I know, did not exist, and this same underground 'accused' Shimon of collaborating with the Germans. I wonder who cared that this event would be recorded in the history of Mezritch by the city's official historian living there today, and it seems likely that his sources were very limited although still quite intriguing." [13]

---

13. Shortly after the German invasion of Poland there was an attempt to organize an underground of youngsters in Mezritch, but the group disintegrated, due to informers.

The Small Escape

The Krzna River, which crossed the city from southeast to northwest, meant freedom for me, representing unlimited spaces and also the pleasures in life. I loved the river during all seasons of the year. In the summer, I swam in its clear waters that spread from horizon to horizon, I paddled in my kayak, and in the magical evenings I hid with my girlfriends among the tall bushes along its banks. In the fall and winter, when its waters froze, I used to skate to my heart's content, or to hike upon the ice with my buddies. In the spring, I stood on the shore and watched the huge ice floes floating past and beating against the bridge pillars, which occasionally buckled under the great load. The river was also a source of livelihood for the city, being its major water supply. The pumps standing along the banks would fill the water wagons of peddlers who made the rounds among households selling water for daily use. The adjoining bath-houses were used for daily washing and, of course, for the Sabbath. I never imagined that the Krzna River would serve as my life's shield, but that is what it became.

Christmas Eve 1942 and I am in the Mezrich Ghetto. The Germans decided to give this day off to all the nationalities. Much to our surprise some of the Jews also enjoyed this free day without work. Not that we received a salary for working in the army camps, but under this awful occupation regular meals along with a place to pass some hours were of utmost importance.

Life in the ghetto was unbearable. The ghetto served not only those of us from the city, but the many inhabitants from the nearby and distant towns who were evicted from their homes. The over-crowding and stuffiness were an in-escapable part of life. The poverty and scarcity were impossible to describe. Legally, food was not to be found. All the products were smuggled into the ghetto by whoever passed by outside the fences, and were purchased through desperate means. The color black and death was dominant everywhere. Whoever did not receive the few calories necessary to sustain him for another day died of starvation, usually alone in the gutter. Many bodies accumulated on the sides of the neglected streets. Each one worried about himself or his family. There was nothing to give, and if there was your family received first.

On the cold and snowy morning of 25 December I awoke relatively early. It was still totally dark, and a quiet permeated the area. Although I could pass the day being idle I dressed and took the small amount of currency I had. I wanted to approach the local Polish market and see if I could buy something. It was just a way to pass the day outside the ghetto. Perhaps I wished to challenge myself, and maybe I wanted to hear news. I knew how to utilize my appearance – light skin, blue/green eyes, and blond hair. Thus I could easily assimilate among the local gentiles.

But even the simple act of being found among the gentiles was not a trivial task. In order to get to the market adjoining the Polish church, I had to leave the ghetto through a breach in the fence, in violation of the rules and regulations. The punishment was well known – death by shooting. I thought that today the Germans would actually reduce their guard duties.

Passing through the fence was easy. On the other side of the fence, near the Great Synagogue, I met Rybak, who was the cousin of my Aunt Rachel's husband. Rybak, who was a carpenter, had also decided to pass part of his time on the Polish side.

I was pleased since I thought that being with someone else there would be some 'action'. Better two than one. However, after the first curve in our path we saw a boy running past us like a madman. "The Germans discovered me", he shouted while passing us.

We didn't manage to comprehend what he had said yet we started running after him. Despite our heavy clothes – the long coat that covered me and the heavy boots that I wore, I leaped after the boy we didn't know and Rybak followed.

The boy raced to the vicinity of the gates of the leather factory nearby the river that had belonged to the Gorman family. He forcibly opened the massive gate made of wood and metal that was in disrepair, and he continued to run towards the river, with me right behind him. From the corner of my eye, I managed to see that Rybak, who had difficulty running, tried his luck by hiding behind the huge gate.

The two Germans who were on our trail raced after us towards the river, leaving Rybak behind them. This time luck was in his favor. Since our trail was lost in the local maze, they climbed onto the roof of a two-story wooden structure along the river, whose rail was removed because of the war, so that they would have an unobstructed view and good vantage over the area.

The boy reached the river, jumped into the freezing water and began to swim in the direction of the opposite bank. Unlike him, I quickly concluded that the safest solution will be to cross the river, but not in the direction of the bank directly opposite us. On the one hand, I didn't want to struggle with the strong current and huge ice chunks. On the other hand, I didn't want to be discovered by the Germans, who could view me from the building on the riverbank, turning me into a sure target against the surrounding whiteness. So I swam to the left with the current along the closer bank towards a curve in the river. The freezing cold of the water, large pieces of ice, and the heavy clothes that I wore didn't make it easier for me. Suddenly I heard a number of shots echoing and afterwards dead silence. I continued to swim while realizing that they would not let me go, and that I must squeeze myself as close as possible to the bank so they could not see me. Moments later I heard the buzzing of bullets that whistled right by me. The ripples caused by these shots frightened me to death. I tried to shrink myself as much as I could and escape in the direction of the bushes so the Germans could not see me. But my slowness was my downfall. I didn't manage to escape. The shots grew and drew closer.

These are my last minutes, I thought to myself. But when the sound of shots quieted down for a while, and I wasn't in the line of sight between the building roof and the river, I quickly left the water and began to run as long as my wind held out towards some abandoned wooden buildings that were in the distance. To say that I ran like a young deer would be exaggerating. The water absorbed by my clothes and boots made it very difficult for me. I looked back from time to time to check if the Germans were closing in on my trail, more precisely the telltale trail left in the snow that I could not camouflage. I tried to run on twigs, straw, and dirt to make it difficult for my pursuers to detect my trail. After several tens of meters I gambled on an abandoned wooden two-story house and entered it. I knew that the Germans would not give up easily.

When I entered the bungalow, I dragged behind me a broken door made of wooden panels, leaned it on the wall leading to the attic and climbed up. From my experience I knew that the owners, if they made typical use of the attic, would surely leave straw for cushioning. When I saw that the attic was indeed filled with straw, I somehow pulled with all my remaining strength the broken door that I had used as a ladder to get up, hid it and myself within the straw and waited.

The voices of the German soldiers were not long in coming. They were heard passing from house to house, from bungalow to shed. I heard them entering the structure where I was hiding. Their voices were clearly audible. Since they suspected that I was in the attic, one soldier lifted the other up on his shoulders. At first I saw fingers, then the palm of a hand, and after that a head wearing a hat. My eyes caught the flash of the German's eyes. I held my breath. For a moment I thought he was swaying, but he steadied himself immediately. Again, he stared in my direction, but stayed transfixed as ice. He looked away from me and stared at the sides of the attic.

"There is nobody here", he said to my surprise. He waited another moment and disappeared from my field of view. The sound of boots on the wooden floor broke the absolute silence.

"Come on", I again heard his voice in the distance. Probably he saw me and let me go, or for an instant I could see but couldn't be seen and managed to blend into the darkness that permeated the attic.

When they departed, a heavy exhaustion fell upon me. Even today, 60 years after the event, I remember that I dreamed about a Paul Muni movie I saw several years before, where he is shown escaping from the local police, then jumps into the river, and saves his breath and his life by using a hollow straw reed. I speculated upon the fate of Rybak and the other boy. Did they remain alive? Had anyone been hit by the shots that I had heard?

When I awoke, it was nightfall and totally dark outside. The surrounding silence let me hear people's voices at a distance. I came down from the attic with a jump and I stared through the bungalow cracks. I saw in the distance a group of Jews who passed between the bungalows to the ghetto. I knew that this was an opportune moment to return to the ghetto that I had left that morning. I joined them in one of the curves on the path and I returned with them to my family in the ghetto.

Meanwhile Rybak had waited several minutes behind the factory gate, and when he saw the Germans running towards the abandoned houses he slipped back to the ghetto and returned to his house.

* * *

"Rybak said that you were probably killed", Zeev told me when I returned home. "He said that he heard a round of rifle-fire and afterwards quiet, so he was sure you were killed", he added. "But probably he didn't wish to cause me worry so he said that perhaps you escaped to one of the Polish villages located nearby". When he heard that perhaps I managed to escape, he went to the police station to poke around for information. Maybe they knew something there.

"One of the boys was killed in the water and must be fetched out", my brother overheard one cop say to his friend.

The police officer sent the Jewish cop Scholeize with a boat to take the dead body out of the water. My brother, who wondered whether I was alive, followed him. When they had recovered the corpse he realized that it wasn't me and thought that maybe I had managed to escape to the Poles. He returned to the police station and asked one of the cops to join him in searching the neighboring villages. The police could circulate outside more freely than just some Jew. After a few hours of searching my brother returned empty-handed from his wandering among the villages. "I was certain that you had been killed" he concluded.

At home I took off all my clothes. As I removed the overcoat I saw that the cloth of the right shoulder was pierced in two places, apparently caused by the bullets the Germans fired at me as I swam in the river. Tzvia, my cousin, carefully removed from my pocket the paper money that I had taken with me in the morning to the market, and spread it on the table to dry.

And so, the Krzna River, in whose waters I so much loved to swirl about during summer days that appeared more distant than ever, had wrapped me in one of its curves and hid me from the German murderers who had tried to shoot me. To my sorrow, the boy who caused our lives to be saved was shot and killed.

My Last *Actzia*

After the fourth *actzia* we decided, Zeev and I, to build a bunker in the house yard. We wanted to build a cover or hiding place in which we could survive for some time. The rumors about the death camps multiplied, and it was obvious to us that whoever was caught would end up in Treblinka.

The most suitable location for a bunker was beneath a wooden structure that served for wood storage, whose entrance was planned to be through the out-house toilet in the yard, a short distance from it. We dug for a month, all the young members of the family, beneath the wood-storage shed and the toilet. The work had to be done secretly. We feared informers most of all. The pales filled with sand that we dispersed at night in locations distant from the house to avoid leaving a trail. We were certain that we were not the only ones doing this, due to the stains of fresh dirt that was spread around the area. The Germans – either they didn't know or they ignored the facts.

When the digging was complete, we wanted to re-enforce the bunker. We looked for a professional, and after several days we hired the services of one of the Jewish carpenters from the ghetto. We smuggled wood beams that he needed to stabilize the bunker ceiling and walls. The work was completed one month later. The bunker was ready.

* * *

"More than likely there will be an *actzia* tomorrow", Zeev said on the First of May, 1943, when he returned from work. "There are unusual activities by the army and police in the vicinity of the city", he added, "Something is about to happen."

As I have said, the city of Mezritch is alongside the main road to the Russian border. Army traffic in both directions was common. But the traffic that Zeev saw, in his words, was really different. Not only was the army involved, but the Gestapo too.[14]

Next morning, on the second of May, the *actzia* began. As soon as we heard the first sounds we decided to enter the bunker.

Entry into the bunker was hasty and my uncle, who was the last to enter, locked the house door and did not take the key with him, a mistake that we didn't stop talking about. We were worried about going out to bring the key because we did not want to be discovered.

We were twelve souls crammed into the crowded space, including the Shainberg family, the Lynn family, the tailor's family from Nasielsk, my brother and I. The tailor decided to leave his two year old baby and not bring him into the bunker for fear that his crying would give us away. Despite the crowding and lack of ability to move in the narrow space, we managed to press together and maintain complete silence.

The bunker was not sealed and we could hear the voices of German soldiers and policeman looking for and actually finding our neighbors in the nearby houses. And then our turn came. At first we heard strong pounding on the door. There was a rough knock and then another knock. They also called for us. When they were not answered the house door was broken in. They understood immediately that we were in the vicinity.

---

14. On the Second and Third of May, 1943 the Germans renewed their search for bunkers in the ghetto. About 4,000 people were caught during this round-up. Hundreds were shot to death in the ghetto itself.

They saw the key in the lock and after a brief search they found the hidden baby. Many policemen and S.S. looked for us. They turned the house upside down and didn't find a thing. After a duration that seemed an eternity, they decided to leave the place. Their goal was to fill a certain quota rather than actually find us. Perhaps we had escaped to the forests?

That afternoon, after they left us alone, I heard an enormous explosion – a noise that violently shook the whole area. Inside the bunker the explosion seemed like an earthquake. We had no idea what was happening. I had never been exposed to such a loud blast or explosion. I dreamed that a German ammunition depot had exploded. Only this would console me. Later it became evident that the Great Synagogue was destroyed. Another blast, smaller, had destroyed the smaller synagogue that was nearby.

At night, when we were still in the bunker, we again heard the voices of searchers. This time the Germans acted smarter. They brought a Jewish neighbor who was passing by and who shouted in Yiddish: "Mr. Lynn, Mr. Lynn, Mr. Lynn, I'm injured, please let me into the bunker". My uncle recognized the voice.

"Should we open?" he whispered in my ear.

"Don't you dare!" I replied immediately. "The Germans are using a trick to try to expose us."

No one managed to sleep that night.

* * *

"Here is the entrance to the bunker", we suddenly heard a voice from outside the next morning. I immediately recognized the voice of one of the female neighbors.

"Get out, get out !" the German soldiers shouted from behind the locked door. Nobody answered or moved.

"If you don't come out, we will throw grenades inside."

We didn't respond. Quiet prevailed for a few minutes and we

hoped that perhaps they thought that they had been mistaken and retreated. But suddenly the bunker door was broken down.

"Get out!", the dogs barked, and they hit our heads with rifle butts. "Get out!"

"How many people are there in the bunker?", the German demanded of my brother Zeev, after he exited and got the rifle butt in his face and a kick to his testicles.

"If you want to know, count for yourself", he answered the policeman.

The policeman took a digging hoe and hit Zeev all over his body. Zeev was bleeding from his swollen face. When I exited immediately after Zeev, I saw the cop hit him as if overcome with obsession. Another soldier hit me in the head with the butt of his rifle. I tried to wipe the blood from my face and I caught a ringing strike. Despite the blood on my eyebrows, and the blinding light that hit my eyes upon going from the darkness into light, I managed to see the neighbor who informed. She stood at the edge of the yard, and stared at us.

When the last of those hiding were outside, a German entered the bunker and checked that no one had remained.

Suddenly a single shot was heard and the girl informer fell lying in her blood, and after a few seconds, another shot was fired at her. "I promised her that if she informs she will remain in the city and not join those being expelled during the *actzia*", the German laughed, "and she indeed remained. A promise must be kept. Right, Hans?" he turned to the soldier next to him.

While receiving deadly blows, we were led to one of the fields in the outskirts of the city, on Brisker Street, the way to the Jewish cemetery. All the Jews caught in the last two days were rounded up in this field. Germans also passed among the Jews and surprised them with their blows.

* * *

133

Our family sat together, close to each other. When I sat down, I pulled on the edge of my shirt and wiped the blood that gushed onto my face. The motion didn't appeal to the soldier near us. He motioned to me, but did not approach me because he was busy troubling someone else.

"I was saved from another strike", I thought to myself.

Chernobroda, the famous artist in town, sat a little ways from my family, holding onto brushes that he wouldn't part with.

"Give me the brushes" a soldier tried to intimidate the artist.

Chernobroda got excited. He tried to hide them under his armpit. I felt that the brushes were as dear to him as his children. The German did not hesitate for a moment and hit Chernobroda's head with a mighty blow. When the blood began to cover his face, the German grabbed from him, with a satanic smile on his face, one of the brushes and started to draw with pleasure on Chernobroda's face with his own blood. "Have your picture", he said and added a kick to the artist's back.

At night we were taken in a long, endless, convoy to the train station. The destination – Treblinka.

The Trip to Treblinka, No – To Maidanek

It was obvious to everybody that this was the end. The last trip from the train station, that served me so often. However, the destination this time – Treblinka. We knew that no one returned from Treblinka.

The Germans, along with the Ukrainian and Polish collaborators, ordered us to climb into the boxcars. They stood at the entrance and squeezed us inside forcibly. I estimate that there were about 150-200 people in the car that I was pushed into. It was a freight car that would normally hold at the most 30-40 people. The car's structure didn't allow any ventilation, and already at the entrance many people peeled off their clothes in order to lighten the oppressive heat.

Those that surrendered even before climbing aboard sat where they had stood. They condemned themselves to death. Absolute surrender.

The stench of vomit, excrement and urine, which filled the closed space caused those few who survived to behave inhumanly. The thirst was so intense, that even the request for me to pee into someone's mouth to moisten his throat was not unreasonable. And other disclosures were rampant, like stealing money from those who had released their soul.

* * *

At this moment, Dad stopped telling his story... He asked me not to record these last events. Despite my many pleas for him to elaborate, he refused.

* * *

"We are not traveling to Treblinka," a voice was heard some time after the train began to move, and perhaps with a note of happiness.

"How do you know?", I heard another voice.

"I jumped from the train during the previous *actzia*, and I'm sure that this is another direction", we heard the answer.

I assumed that from the length of the path, the changing of tracks, and the many stops, one could determine that this direction did not lead to Treblinka.

A relief? I thought. Luck? Actually there lay before me many dead people. How could one think about luck.

"Maidanek", someone said, "I'm sure that we are traveling to Maidanek".

We knew very little about Maidanek. We knew that it was also a death camp, like Treblinka, but it was also a transfer camp, and even a work camp.

Perhaps there is a chance? I thought to myself.

When I climbed onto the freight car I tried to remain near the door. Even when I was pushed inside I grabbed onto the threshold and stayed there. If I am forced to the center of the car, the chance of escaping is minimal. If I can stay near the door, there is a chance to jump, I thought to myself. In the ghetto we heard about those who had jumped and returned to Mezritch or escaped to the forest and joined the partisans.

During the last period in the ghetto I always carried a pair of pliers and a small saw. I knew that these tools could serve me in many situations, like breaching fences or unlocking doors. Who knows what the day would bring?

Now, in the freight car, maybe I would use them.

And so, immediately after the train started to move we began – my brother Zeev, Pini Buchovsky, and myself – each one in turn, to saw the heavy hook that locked the door. The immense heat, the sweat that gushed, the unbearable human crush and the terrible stink did not make it easier on us, to put it mildly. But we were determined to break open the door, come what may. In fact, even before we reached Lukov the door broke open.

"I'm opening the door", Zeev said, "move a bit", and little by little the door opened and light flooded into the dark freight car.

Gunshots suddenly rang out. They were aimed at the opening. It turned out that the Germans had positioned Ukrainian POWs (from General Vlasov's unit) on the roof of the boxcar and they performed their guard duty faithfully. The rifles were pointed diagonally inside.

My brother, who opened the door and stood in the first row, was immediately hit in the arm and fell bleeding directly into my arms. Others, who saw the door flung wide open, took advantage of the opportunity and began jumping from the train. I have no idea if there were any survivors from this jump. I remember that my friend, Sonia Kamin, jumped from the car. She managed to part from me with a word and jumped. I saw a bullet blast her head while she was still in the air, a bullet fired by a damn Ukrainian soldier.

Zeev was hit by a poisoned dumdum bullet. These bullets were favorites among the Germans. Every scratch caused death to whomever it hit. The poison immediately began to spread in Zeev's blood. We both knew that these were his last moments. The boxcar partially emptied of those living travelers, such that I could find a relatively comfortable position, as Zeev leaned upon me. Despite great efforts, I did not succeed in stopping the bleeding.

The train stopped in Lukov. No one knew if this was a

planned stop or an emergency halt, due to the escape, but this didn't interest me.

The Ukrainian soldiers came down from the roof and immediately went to the wide-open door. One of them pointed his rifle at us. "Who opened the door?", roared the soldier, "who was it?".

My brother, with so much blood gushing from his arm, got up without hesitation using his remaining strength, and stepped forward. "I did", Zeev said, and pride sounded in his voice. "I did", he said again.

The Ukrainian stared at him and called immediately to the S.S. soldier. "He broke open the door", the Ukrainian pointed at Zeev. "He's the one!"

"I'm about to die", said Zeev, "but you, the Germans and Ukrainians, will hang by the balls." The German didn't bat an eyelash, aimed his rifle at my brother's head, and fired. The German didn't give a damn that a row of people stood behind my brother and could be injured from the shot.

Zeev collapsed. I approached him, and hugged him. I lowered him carefully onto the floor of the car. His warm blood gushed onto my chest and mixed with my sweat. The Germans closed the car door and the train started off in the direction of Lublin, and from there to the train station adjacent to Maidanek. On the evening of the fourth of May 1943 we arrived at the camp.

When they ordered us to climb down from the cars, I lowered my brother, and afterwards my dead uncle Baruch Lynn, who was among those who gave up hope at the beginning of the trip. He had avoided witnessing Zeev's murder. The number of dead during the trip was great and it was very difficult to identify them. Joseph Finkelstein, who was shot in the leg back in Lukov, asked me to help him, but the futility that I felt, and the Germans pushing me, prevented my getting involved.

* * *

When already at Maidanek for several days, and after the first *selectzia* had me working in the clothing warehouse, I became very excited when I recognized my brother's clothes. The shirt was stained with blood. In the shirt pocket I found one of the identification documents that they issued for Zeev in Mezritch. I decided to keep the document no matter what.

When we left the clothing warehouse we underwent a light search. The document was in my hand. That night I found a piece of tin. With great effort I managed to bend the metal and make a sort of small box. I folded the document and the picture within, and I placed them inside the box. I rehearsed in my heart the decision to keep them no matter what.

When asked if I had the time to mourn over my brother who was murdered in my arms, I reply that the Germans made sure that no one had time to think about anything.

Mr. Death

One must call the Maidanek death camp "Mr. Death". I don't know if the name Maidanek has a verbal description. It doesn't really matter to me. For me Maidanek means death. The value of a Jewish life was less than a garlic skin, since there is still a use for the peel, but a dead Jew represents a transportation problem whose solution must be planned. The cheapness of life in Maidanek was notorious. The Jews served as marbles for play by the S.S. soldiers and their collaborators – the Ukrainians, the Poles and others.

I often felt that there was competition among the Germans as to who would propose the craziest idea at their regularly scheduled lavish dinners. The camp inhabitants served as playthings to implement these violent ideas.

For example, every morning and afternoon, as we left for work ordered outside the camp, the officer controlling us would announce: "Group so-an-so consisting of 80 prisoners is leaving for work".

The answer that he received in crisp German, in a loud and clear voice, that everyone would hear, was: "You must return to camp with half that number".

The free hand that the officers and soldiers in charge had to cut down whoever their whim fancied and using whatever method, didn't surprise anyone. In fact, there were groups where the Germans would exterminate anyone they wanted just like that. They didn't need to search for a reason. As someone who remained alive I don't understand how I managed to pass these daily *selectzias*.

The simplest method for killing was a bullet in the victim's head. No excuse needed. The German approached, often-times during a conversation with a friend or work foreman, draw a pistol and shoot. Sometimes the officer was angry because they were not working fast enough, and other times he was angry because they worked too fast. Sometimes he was telling a joke, and other times he would ask a question and answer it himself by shooting.

One of the methods that the officers discussed at dinner was apparently how to mass exterminate without wasting valuable resources – a pistol bullet. The technique of beating around the victim's head was very common, but the blood that spurted from him would dirty the clothes of the striker, what a pity... The "see-saw" was the worst for us, but the most amusing for them of course. If two S.S. soldiers approached you with a beam, you knew that you were the next victim. In order not to become soiled, they ordered the victim to lie down on his back, place the wood beam on his neck, and began to see-saw up and down while the victim's neck served as the pivoting axle. They would continue this way for their pleasure until the victim's soul departed, and then moved on to the next random victim. Often one could hear the cracking of neck bones during the "see-sawing" up and down. The rounds of laughter that were swallowed in the victim's screams still echo in the ears of many of us until today. There is no lack of reasons to hate the Germans. But the "see-saw" is a great part of the hatred that still churns inside me towards the German people.

* * *

I arrived in Maidanek a day after I left Mezritch. A trip that usually lasted four hours took 24 hours, a whole day! When we entered the death camp gates, whose black watchtowers ringing the portal represented the entry to hell, we passed by the shining swimming pools used by the camp guards. Even though we knew that water contained chlorine, our falling onto the pools was unavoidable. Despite the shots and wholesale killing, the number of water guzzlers didn't diminish. The thirst was unbearable, and I wasn't surprised that many decided to sacrifice their lives for a little disinfected water.

I endured the first *selectzia* in my life immediately upon entering the death camp. No one understood the meaning of the division between right and left. Meir and Masha Gittel were steered towards the left, and Rivka and I remained on the right side. Seeing that our family became divided, I moved with Rivka to the left side, to reunite with my family. The S.S. soldiers, who despised our transition, caught Rivka and I, beat us, and moved us forcibly to the right – back again. Only afterwards did we comprehend that right meant life to the Germans. But what kind of life? This I was to understand in the coming years.

After the *selectzia*, the undressing, the shower and receiving color-marked clothing, we went to the office area. There we received numbers that were sewed onto each of our shirts and pants. Likewise we received numbered identification tags. The order at each stage of absorption was maintained by veteran Jewish prisoners from Czechoslovakia. Later on I learned that 200 souls arrived in the transport from Czechoslovakia and only 20 remained who worked as orderlies.

While waiting for a number, I asked one of the guards: "Perhaps you know something about my brother Naphtali Brezniak? I know that he was sent to Maidanek".

"If you don't shut up you'll join your brother", was the answer I received from that Czechoslovakian Jew.

With the registration process done we were divided into

groups of 500 people. I was placed within field[15] number 4 in shack #12, which was the last in a line and very close to the eastern fence. The shacks were enormous and the smell reeking from the walls was unbearable. The bench-planks that were covered with straw rose up three levels. Minutes after we entered the shack we were called to line up and become acquainted with the camp rules. The thousand people who occupied field number 4 were arranged in triplets. The camp and field officers stood on a central platform. Erected alongside the platform were four hanging poles with thick rope swinging from them. Four camp residents were standing, one near the base of each pole, and in our presence a hanging rope was placed around each one's neck.

Am I about to witness an execution? I asked myself.

The Germans did not stop explaining the camp rules, until they came to the punishment. The victims did not know, until the rope was removed from their necks, that this time they are only being used as examples. At the end of the demonstration it was clear to us the fate of anyone who disobeyed an order, rule or regulation.

* * *

The daily routine was monotonous: we were roused at 5:30 for discipline exercises – marching in triplets from that hour until darkness fell. There were no regular meals, and it goes without saying there were no fixed hours for meals. At times the food didn't arrive, and often the food that came was not enough for the whole camp. The food and getting it were obviously the central issues occupying us most of our waking hours during the day and night. During sleep we could only dream about

---

15. The Maidanek camp was divided into fenced-in areas that were nicknamed *fields* (Polish).

food. Only when there is none, and the stomach grumbles, does one understand the true meaning of having food.

I hated the long disciplinary drills. There was nothing to do with us and therefore we were forced to walk endlessly and without purpose. When the first occasion arose that required a few prisoners for work, I took advantage of my connections with the block leader – *blockaltesta* – that I knew from Mezritch. With his aid I managed to be among 15 that were spared the drills and placed in shack #1 to sort clothing.

* * *

All the clothing from the prisoners taken to Maidanek, whether they were alive or dead, was sorted in this shack. Our task was to pass over each article and search for hidden treasures. Several barrels were placed in the center of the shack into which we had to throw whatever property we found. And we found quite a lot. The Kapo in charge of us was a Polish nobleman who was a political prisoner[16]. The clothing came to us partially unraveled, apparently having undergone a preliminary search on the way to the warehouse. Despite this, one could still find in them money and other valuables that were hidden in the folds and buttons of the cloth.

I already described my excitement upon finding Zeev's shirt. When I found small amounts of money I threw them into the barrel, but the larger sums I hid in my clothes or shoes and smuggled outside. The punishment of death for smuggling like this did not inhibit me. The Polish Kapo didn't especially enforce authority. He was an easy-going person.

"Is it worth losing your life for such a measly sum of money?" he asked me when he saw my delay in tossing 20 zloty into the barrel.

---

16. A few year ago I learned that he belonged to Jacqueline Kennedy's family.

"I was confused for a moment", I answered him, and immediately tossed the sum into the barrel near him. A noble soul, I thought to myself when it became apparent that I hadn't been punished.

When S.S. soldiers arrived at the shack without advanced warning, we feared searches that were often conducted on our bodies.

Once I found a gold watch and without hesitation I hid it in my underwear and later gave it to Shula Wainer. Another time I found a roll of dollars, which also stayed in my shirt until it went to Bunim Wasserman.

There were four shacks on the western side of field number 4 that were isolated by barbed wire. Craftsmen who worked in sorting hair bristles for manufacturing brushes were living there. The residents of Mezritch were well known for this expertise, and members of my family did this work before the war. The Germans took advantage of these skills, and a factory for sorting hair bristles was set up in field number 4 with three shacks alongside it. In one of these shacks lived families, in the second shack bachelors, and in the third shack unmarried women. These people, who were isolated from the rest of the field's population, worked in the factory. Bunim Wasserman, my friend from Mezritch, was there with his mother.

* * *

At the beginning of my work in the sorting department I found a girdle belt with pockets. I wore the belt on my stomach, and that evening I passed it to Bunim to give to his mother. In the following days I passed large sums of money to Bunim for his mother to guard.

One day, during the sorting process I heard a knock, or more exactly a weak thud, on the sorting table. Slowly and carefully lest I was caught, I searched with my hands for the source of the noise. While manipulating the garment's cloth that was already turned inside-out I felt a solid mass between my fingers. I tightly grasped the bulge as if to make it disappear. I felt something moving within the mass. Diamonds, I thought to myself. I ripped the bulge from the shirt while heavily coughing and I quickly stuffed it into my shirt. The sack of diamonds, that was hidden within a large cloth pocket, was given to Baruch Mordechai Reinwein. I also managed to give large amounts of money during this period to Rybak, from my family, who arrived at Maidanek from Trevniki.

And what could one do with money and diamonds? The forced laborers who worked in the hair bristle factory were in contact with Polish workers who came to the factory from outside the camp. The prisoners could buy food from them with the money. The bread was outrageously expensive but could be bought for large sums of money.

My work sorting clothing was an unstoppable source of great sums of money that was used to buy bread and other food. This was a big relief to me and my family. Even the Kapo enjoyed the money we found.

Six innocent weeks of work sorting clothing and accumulating wealth on the side were over and the process stopped. I was forced to return to the drills that I hated. Walking around without purpose drove me out of my mind. There was no chance for improvisation. I always had to be there and there was no where to hide. The field was open, and how often could you go to the bathroom? Worst of all, the stash of money dwindled.

* * *

Women lived in field number 5, which was on the north side of field number 4 where I slept. Between the two fields there was an enormous clearing used for storing the coal used in the camp. The men in field number 4 would speak to the women of field number 5 by shouting, despite the mood of the German guards who couldn't stand any noise coming from the Jewish prisoners. In order to stop the disturbance and to prevent any communication, they shot at those standing by the fences. Those running from the fence were not always fast enough, so there were many victims on both sides – men and women. But after only a few minutes, again one could hear shouts from one side to another while they slowly approached the fence, until another rifle round was heard dispersing the people once more.

To my satisfaction, after a relatively short interval of meaningless marching I was brought to a group that went to work outside the camp. We were occupied primarily with digging that seemed pointless to us, but the activity and the opportunity to meet civilians changed the daily routine entirely. The excavation was boring but passing the time was more reasonable than marching.

Once, when I was in the field, I met Rivka Scheinberg. Rivka removed a piece of bread from the folds of her dress and gave it to me. The following is the list of sins and transgressions that were committed during the banal interlude of a meeting between a man and his cousin: Rivka hid money in her boot which helped her buy the bread from one of the civilians who worked there; Rivka and I met against the rules; Rivka passed me food which was forbidden. Each of these acts, if discovered by those watching over us, would have ended both our lives.

If I'm asked why I did this, I say that at this stage every act was intuitive, without deep thought. The drive to survive acted only instantaneously. Except for the instant gratification no act had an influence on the future. We knew that the Germans were not searching reasons to end life. The transgression cannot stand up to any measure of logic, reason, or rational thought.

* * *

I recall that during a certain period I tried to change my work place and enter the hair-bristle factory. There was a different order in the factory. The food arrived on time and the prisoners were not beaten by their guards – two factors that significantly changed the existence in this awful camp. One way to change status was by paying money. Since I had accumulated enough money while working at the clothes sorting shack (although it was not with me), I asked Bunim to provide enough money for me to join these factory workers. We arranged a time to meet by the fence. Excited by the prospect of changing my status I arrived at the meeting place somewhat earlier than the appointed hour. When I saw Bunim, I counted his steps as if something huge was about to happen. Bunim walked slowly, hesitating slightly. He wasn't late, which was a good sign.

"My mother was robbed." Bunim whispered hesitantly.

My world darkened around me. I didn't know what to say, and certainly did not know what to do.

"We'll both be hanged", I blurted out in desperation.

"I don't care any more", I heard him whisper, after which he turned and left.

I stared at him a long time and I clenched my fists. And what else could I do? I was certain that my days in this place were numbered and I wouldn't be able to avoid Mr. Death who was hovering and collecting to his bosom thousands every day. The last line of defense that I dreamed about had disintegrated and actually vanished before my eyes.

I assume that Bunim lied to me. He had enough reasons to lie. His status in the enclosed area was excellent. Money wasn't lacking. His family was with him and there was food in sufficient quantities compared to Maidanek. And what could I offer him – nothing, zero. I wasn't significant in his eyes anymore. It was easier for him to guard the cash and the security than to share it with a friend. Bunim remained in Maidanek and during the "Harvest Festival" was placed in a gas chamber along with the rest of the factory workers, and evaporated.

* * *

One day the Germans instructed a group of girls to uproot weeds in the buffer zone between the camp fences, work that could be described as reasonable. But the Germans ordered these girls to work while squatting in a frog's position. Whoever was found sitting on the buffer-ground, or bending over instead, would be punished. Since uprooting weeds in this position was impossible, the number of girls who were punished continued to increase. In the end the camp commander decided to punish all the inhabitants by ordering every motion in the camp to be done at a run. It was forbidden to see anyone standing or walking. And remember that we were forced to run after an exhausting work day. And who had the energy? I don't know how I did it, but I remember that for two weeks we ran as if possessed by hysteria, and the punishment for disobeying this order – the same punishment that Abel received from Cain.

The minor punishment, in retrospect, did not satisfy the camp commander's needs, and he decided to do something. After work we were divided into two groups. Each group was positioned on the other side of the camp. The task was simple. The prisoners were forced to collect gravel, put it in their hats and run to the other side of the camp while both hands held their hats. You finished one direction, you dumped the gravel near the fence, and you again collected gravel and returned it to the other side. Sounds terrible? Not really. There was a catch to it. The commander placed human "poles" in the midst of the field that we ran across, whose sole purpose was to interfere with the run. Therefore it was impossible to run straight

149

across. Occasionally the "poles" would beat the runners with clubs or whips, and often demonstrated unusual mobility and prevented the prisoner from running by whipping and beating him on the face and body. These same "poles" were prisoners or Ukrainian collaborators and S.S. soldiers, who simply wanted to take part in the day's enjoyment.

Is it possible to describe what was revealed to God's eyes in that same part of Maidanek that he viewed one afternoon in 1943? Many of the prisoners were lying dead on the expansive field, injured, unconscious, while their brothers were running from side to side between human animals who barked, bit, and tore their flesh.

* * *

As noted, I lived in a shack near the camp fence. One night we awoke in panic from rounds of gunfire that did not cease. It's hard to estimate how long the shots were heard, but to the shack inhabitants it sounded like an eternity. The shots were actually fired along the shack wall and we were worried that the Germans would shoot in the direction of the shack itself. The shack officer forbade us from coming down from the wooden plank beds to investigate what was happening.

The next morning we didn't see anything unusual. The rumor that passed from lips to ears told of a group of Russian pilots who attempted to escape using a ladder, which they threw onto the camp fence near our shack. All the pilots were shot dead, the area was cleaned that night by other prisoners, who were then led to the nearby gas chamber as a sign of gratitude.

Escape from the camp was almost impossible. Even the one successful escape ended a few days later with the hanging of the escapee. And this is how it happened: the neighboring farmers collected the excrement that gathered surrounding the shacks to enrich their land, by fertilizing the fields. Each evening a Polish farmer arrived with a horse and wagon, and with the help of several prisoners collected the secretions into appropriate barrels. One day, one of the barrels remained unfilled and one of the prisoners snuck inside. As the wagon exited the camp none of the camp guards dared to climb up onto the wagon to check the contents. The smell repulsed from the wagon anyone in the near vicinity and far away as well. Despite the stench, the prisoner managed to reach the nearby city, but he was caught during one of the *actzias* and returned to the camp to be hanged immediately.

Whip lashing, which was the classic punishment, was administered in the field on a special table. It was an amazing German design that reflected their famous efficiency. Wanting to remain clean, the one who whipped laid the victim on the special table in order to whip at an appropriate height without bending over, thus to see only the behind of the beaten prisoner. The table was tilted, such that the victim's back and head were placed on the surface at an optimum angle, the knees were bent slightly, and the rear-end stuck out exactly opposite the whip of the beater. The victim had no way to move.

Human engineering at its peak.

* * *

During my last weeks at Maidanek I worked in excavation outside the camp. The work was done under civilian managers who came from nearby Lublin. Trade with these same civilians was almost unrestricted. Whoever had the means bought food from them, smuggled it into the camp, and sold it to other prisoners.

One day in August I received a few zlotys from Baruch Mordecai Reinwein in order to buy rolls (he received the money from me when I worked in clothing sorting). That day I was in the digging crew with two other prisoners. Towards afternoon a Pole approached me and asked if I wanted to buy rolls. I purchased 14 rolls and a half liter of vodka from him. The rolls were wrapped in paper, and I put the vodka bottle into a separate paper bag. The two co-workers each received a roll for one zloty (I didn't do business with them). I hid the remaining 12 rolls in a pit and the bottle of vodka in a separate location. When I finished hiding the vodka bottle I raised my head and my eyes saw black. I saw the same Pole who did business with me conversing with the foreman.

He's squealing on me, I thought. Indeed, the foreman reached the pit, turned directly towards me and asked: "Did you buy rolls?"

"Yes", I answered. I realized that he knew about it. I answered affirmatively without hesitation and immediately gave him two rolls.

Only moments later an S.S. soldier in charge of the site approached me and asked: "Who is doing business with civilians?"

Silence.

And again, in a louder voice: "Who is doing business with civilians?"

Silence.

And this time as a scream: "Who is doing business with civilians?"

Silence.

The two others told me: "We won't give our heads for you."

I immediately raised my hand. I was sure that I wouldn't manage to lower it. The German ordered me to get out of the pit and he gave me 10 lashes with his whip.

"Where are the rolls?"

I descended into the pit, dug, recovered the wrapped rolls, and gave them to him as if it was the dearest treasure that I possessed.

"Where's the chocolate?"

"I didn't buy chocolate".

"Do you have money?"

"No".

The German stared at me, ripped the number stitched on my shirt and found several zloty. He turned and whipped me another ten times.

"Do you have more money?"

"Yes", I bent and withdrew some more zloty from my shoe.

He held my money in his hand and counted it: "How much money did you have?"

I answered him.

"How many rolls did you buy?"

I told him.

"Where are the missing rolls?"

I told him that I had sold two rolls to two girls who had passed by.

"Can you identify them?"

"No".

Ten more lashes cut me immediately.

"How much did they pay you?"

I told him.

When he understood how much money I had he began to think. I had made no mistake. Everything matched up. The validity of my story really angered him and I felt the satisfaction of his whip 20 more times.

I remained at the excavation site without rolls, money, or strength, but with the searing memory of 50 lashes. The soldier disappeared.

After a short while they assembled us and we marched in the direction of the camp. I trudged at the end of the procession. I knew that no good would come of it. Before I entered the camp I saw that the group commander was looking for me and he stepped alongside me. He held an open letter and asked me if I knew German. When I answered in the affirmative he gave me the letter. I silently read and understood: the number of hours I that had left to live were limited. The letter stated that I did business with a civilian, and this proved my attempts to escape, for which I was to be harshly punished. The letter was intended for the commander of field number 4.

"What will you give me if I don't deliver this letter to its destination?" The group commander surprised me by asking.

"A half-liter of vodka", I answered quickly. I hadn't given myself an opportunity to digest the question, much less the answer.

His eyes lit up. It was as if all his senses were focused on the impending swig of vodka. "When?" he asked.

"This evening", I replied, "When we return from work".

I imagined the bottle of vodka that was lying in the dusty heap.

Indeed, torn pieces of the letter remained outside the camp fence. The fear of death disappeared for a moment, but I had two more critical problems confronting me: one, finding the vodka bottle and smuggling it into camp, and two, wondering if we would go out this afternoon to work at the same location.

We were called to return to work in the afternoon. An optimistic sign was the fact that the group commander was replaced, so I could have more time to find the bottle. Fortunately, we arrived at the same site and were divided into the same work crews. I approached where I had hidden the bottle and couldn't find it. In desperation, I began digging around the area very quickly. It was useless. A cold chill spread within my body. Although I was digging very earnestly, my body was covered with the coldest sweat. My pulse was erratic and my breath was short. There was no trace of the bottle or the wrapping paper. It was as if the earth had swallowed it.

"Perhaps the earth hasn't swallowed it?", I turned to my two crew members and asked where the bottle had gone. The answer that I received angered me: "We threw it away because we were afraid."

"In which direction did you throw it?"

"That way!" Each one pointed in a different direction.

I had no choice but to begin looking for the bottle or its broken remains. That whole afternoon I turned the area upside down – for nothing. The clods of earth pitied me. I knew that I had nowhere to return to. Towards evening I returned to the camp, fearing that the officer would search for me. I tried to avoid my shack so that he wouldn't find me. A rumor about a transport of 1,000 people that was supposed to leave the following morning perked me up. They didn't say to where, but the possibility of legally leaving Maidanek and a certain death sentence excited me very much. I tried every possible means to join the transport. I turned to Shula Wiener who worked in the brush-bristle factory. I told her what had happened to me and I asked her if she knew where this transport was going.

"The destination is Auschwitz", she said. "I will help you leave Maidanek", she added.

* * *

Occasionally, S.S soldiers traveled through the camp in search of volunteers for various jobs. After a while the veterans realized that they were filling quotas for the gas chambers. In the beginning many volunteered, but afterwards their numbers continually decreased and the Germans had to apply force. One time several S.S. soldiers came around looking for 20 electricians. It seemed obvious to me that this was really about gas chamber quotas, although after the war I met one of those volunteers who spent the entire war-time in a transformer factory in Germany. This time I suspected that the transport was really destined for the gas chambers. I became less suspicious after talking to Shula, who had connections among those responsible for the brush-bristle factory where she worked (Shula had befriended a German warden who was a political prisoner and who opposed Hitler's regime).

The transport of 1,000 men was combined with the transport of 1,000 women from field number 4. Rivka Scheinberg, my cousin, was among them. They concentrated the women in shack #1 within field number 4, where I worked sorting clothing. When I saw that Rivka was in the group I made an effort to enter the shack. When permitted to enter I searched for her among the 1,000 women and I finally found her. Rivka and I stood hugging, locked arm-in-arm, for a long time and cried. The silence that accompanied our crying continued quit a while. It appeared to me that this was the first time in quite a while that I had really cried, with tears.

Towards evening, the women were evacuated from field number 4. The Germans were concerned that the men and women would mingle together. And where could they be brought to if not to the gas chambers? That space was large enough to contain such a big group of women. Four women from the group, who suspected that the transport would evaporate in the camp's gas ovens, escaped and hid in the bathrooms. The headcount revealed that they were missing and the Germans began an intense search, that concluded with their discovery and punishment in an original way – 25 lashes for each one.

I escaped the punishment of the group commander to whom I promised the half-liter. To where? The following morning I found myself on the Auschwitz ramp with Dr. Mengele standing opposite me.

Stopover at Auschwitz

There was no end to surprises. The transport from Maidanek to Auschwitz was organized. In other circumstances I would even say respectable: this time 60 of us sat on the box car floor, the same box car into which 200 people were squashed after the *actzia*. We even received food. Unbelievable.

When we arrived at Auschwitz we underwent a *selectzia*.

I didn't recognize the name Mengele until after the war. But he was there. During our *selectzia* the Germans were looking for diseased and dysfunctional people. Only a few people failed the "acceptance test", were removed from the transport and sent to another location. Most of us, who had already passed the previous *selectzia* in Maidanek, continued in the absorption line.

We were led to a hall where we undressed, were disinfected within a barrel, showered, and were given camp clothing. I was still carrying my brother's picture inside the small tin box that I made. And the small package containing the picture passed undetected during this stage of absorption.

They settled us within a transfer block, a sort of isolation pen, for four days. Four days in which we could circulate freely in the vicinity. No one harassed us. No one bothered us.

"Come down, come out into the field!" the call was heard at the block entrance on the third morning of our stay.

I went out with everybody to the formation field. We stood

in one mass before the raised platform, "Arrange yourselves in alphabetical order", the command barked from the loudspeaker.

Within several minutes 1,000 men were running about, determining the first letters of everyone's last name and standing like disciplined soldiers in proper order. Our fear of the Germans was great, and they could be seen standing on the platform glowing with satisfaction as we swiftly executed their order. One thousand men ran around – I don't even want to say what we must have looked like.

"Each of you will receive a note with a number," the loudspeaker announced, "You must keep the note." Indeed, we stood in formation and someone stuffed a note displaying a number into my hand. I was intent on keeping it. What was it for? Nobody knew nor told us.

Four days after we had arrived we passed another *selectzia*. This *selectzia* was different. We descended to the formation grounds and stood in rows. At the time I didn't know the purpose. It seemed too clean. It wasn't accompanied by beatings. The S.S. officers and soldiers were joined by civilians that stared at us. They examined us according to criteria known only to them. Afterwards I realized that this *selectzia* was intended to channel forced laborers to the work camp Buna situated nearby Auschwitz-Birkenau. Next to Buna was the A.G. Farben factory – an enormous factory that worked completely for the German army in every sector that one could imagine: generating liquid fuel from coal, processing gas that was pumped from crushed earth, manufacturing pipes, reconditioning tanks, processing raw materials and more.

We stood in formation as laborers at Auschwitz. Workers captured by the Germans. It became known later that they wanted to make an easy profit off our backs. Profits that A.G. Farben extracted from forced labor, and many other factories followed suit. We, and others like us, were a skilled labor pool that was acquired cheaply by the industrialists from the S.S.

Of course, their products were sold at full price to the German authorities. Someone had to finance, to operate, and to lubricate the wheels of the Nazi war and death machine. And who actually enabled this? We, the forced laborers did.

We were transported from Auschwitz to Buna in trucks, a 15 minute trip. "Stand in one row!" We were commanded while getting out of the trucks. "The row must be straight!" the local officer screamed. And that's the way it was. "You must keep the notes that you received!" he warned us.

Only when I approached the head of the line did I understand the meaning and content of the note. In one of the offices they seared that number on my left forearm. The number 127942 is tattooed forever on my arm. And what does the soldier do if he makes a mistake burning the tattoo? He is also human. He erases. And how do you erase a tattoo? You draw a line and sear a new number below the wrong number.

Our humanity had disappeared long before – from now on we were only numbers. The number 127942 was to accompany me from that moment onward.

Buna Camp

The next 17 months passed between the prisoner's camp and the work sites of A.G. Farben situated nearby the camp. At first I lived in block 17 and later I was moved to block 40.

I never thought that there was work that people could describe as back-breaking. Only after that first day of work did I understand what was written in the bible, when it described the Jewish people's labor in Egypt under Pharaoh's rule. Gathering mud (mortar) from pools and loading it onto boxcars was my first encounter with the Buna forced-labor camp. It was hard work that always demanded anyone's utmost strength.

The German soldiers, wanting to be amused, forced all of us to move to and from the boxcars as one entity, so that it would look like something united and perhaps surreal. Whoever didn't obey the discipline of sticking together – to pick up the mud, to run to the boxcar and unload, everything done as one, orchestrated like a concert – caught blows that were often terrible. Spivak, my friend from Mezritch, who couldn't maintain his strength doing this exhausting work, was shot on site, and at the end of this draining labor, we were forced to carry his body several kilometers back to camp. The number going out had to equal the number returning, we were told on leaving – alive or dead. Contrary to what was said at Maidanek.

One evening, when I dragged myself to the camp, I met a Jew named Wolman who worked as an electrician. "Is it possible to join your group?" I asked, "I'm actually an electrician with diplomas – a certified electrician", I added.

"What can you contribute, to someone else who can help?" Wolman asked. What could I give at that point? In fact I didn't have anything and I had no way to get anything.

"I haven't anything to give!" I said. And that ended the conversation.

At the end of the following day, after more back-breaking work, I convinced myself on the march back to Buna that this was to be my last day. I searched for Wolman in the camp.

"I have gold" I said to a surprised Wolman.

"Gold?" he wondered. "From where do you have gold?"

"I have some." I answered. "I'll give it to you, on condition that the work is guaranteed".

Wolman said that gold would solve the problem.

The next day, after many difficulties, I managed to extract the gold bridge that was in my mouth, a bridge I had made before the war and had almost forgotten about. In this state, when I had been praying every night not to wake up the next morning, giving a gold bridge was nothing. Perhaps it could even improve my work place and chance to survive.

"Here's the gold," I told Wolman when we met behind the block, near the bathroom. Wolman, who was in the sought-after *Commando* 9, unit was surprised that I gave it to him. He stared at the piece of gold as if holding a real treasure. When I smiled he understood from where I dredged the precious metal.

"I'll operate quickly with the proper people." He promised and disappeared.

A day passed, and then another day, and a week passed by as well, and I still found myself mining mud from the polluted pools; nothing changed.

"Tomorrow." Wolman said when he saw me. "Tomorrow will be better".

How many tomorrows does a person have to pass for his

dream to come true? The wound in my mouth had already scabbed and the promise was not fulfilled. Time went by. My weight dropped and I felt my strength dwindling. Only the thought that a better tomorrow might come kept me alive.

One day, without connection to the bridge of hope that was fading away, I heard at the prisoner's assembly the following announcement: "We are looking for certified electricians and electrician's assistants." Electrical work in all its variations was a desirable job. Dozens responded to the call and many were imposters. I also signed up and stated that I was a certified electrician.

This time the goddess of luck worked in my favor. I was included in *Commando* 27 that was established that day and included 20 electricians, 19 fakes and only one who possessed a real diploma - me.

And so, without a gold bridge, I built a bridge of hope.

* * *

In the beginning I was assigned to work with an electrician, a Polish civilian. I soon understood the reality of my situation, and I'm not referring to the factory work. Most of the limited energy that I had left was invested, like many others, in the search for addition nourishment.

It was obvious to each forced laborer that within a certain duration, short for one person and relatively long for another, starvation would triumph and the body would not withstand its load. Therefore, like many others, I looked for other sources of food. As an electrician I could make contact with civilians. And here I was working with a Polish civilian.

This civilian lived freely outside the camp. He would arrive every morning to work and return every evening to his home nearby. What could be better? There was nothing like it in camp. Other forced-laborers, who knew that I worked with a

162

civilian and that there was a chance to get something extra, didn't leave me alone. Whoever could, asked to be part of the "food chain". An undershirt for a piece of bread. Several shirts for salami. A pair of shoes for cigarettes or a bottle of wine, and so on. Overnight I became not only an electrician but a merchant. To tell the truth, the trading began to flourish. The following days appeared quite rosy.

With the coming winter and its cold nights, I noticed that there was a demand for electric heating elements. I asked the Polish fellow I worked with – Yanek was his name – if he could purchase several heating elements for me in town, which I could sell to Germans (German civilians working in the factory – not soldiers), or even install within broken heaters. When he agreed, I began to collect money. I could raise it by trading excess clothing that I sold to civilians.

When I had enough money, I asked Yanek to make good on his promise and purchase the heating elements for me. When I received them I gave him his due and then hid the elements in a corner at work. But when I returned to that spot afterwards the heating elements had disappeared. I was enraged and turned the place upside down, but it was useless.

My suspicions fell on Yanek. Only he was aware of my hiding places. In fact we had been working together for several weeks.

I approached him, fuming with anger, and said: "Yanek, I want you to return the heating elements to me. If you don't return them, we are both going".

Yanek saw that I was quite agitated.

We both knew that business of any kind was forbidden in the camp. If I just informed the authorities that I traded with him – his fate would be like mine. After only a few hours the threat worked – I got all the heating elements back from Yanek himself.

As stated, dealings of any kind in the factory were strictly forbidden. The Poles feared the Germans – both the soldiers and the citizens – and so business between them was never considered. As a result, it was easier for both sides, the German citizens and the Polish citizens, to actually do business with the prisoners. It was assumed that these dealings would not be disclosed to the authorities. If they wished, the German citizens could always falsely accuse a prisoner but they usually did not.

* * *

A few days after the incident, Yanek didn't come to work. That day there was a review of the electrical work by the engineering department. The German engineer in charge of the inspection arrived at the site, inspected, didn't ask any questions and said to me: "You have to dismantle all the work that the Pole did, I don't want to see that Polish pig here again. You will fix it." he ordered me.

"I don't have a tool box." I said.

The engineer made a gesture, and the next day I received a tool box with a lock, not small feat for a Jewish prisoner in Buna.

* * *

Food in any form was the center of our lives. Everything in the camp and work circulated around the meager amount of calories that we received in an orderly yet humiliating way; whoever could, acquired additional calories through wheeling and dealing – equally demeaning. The food distributors were lucky people who had access to the civilians who worked in the vicinity.

As a professional electrician I had two obvious advantages. First of all, I could move among the factory buildings almost without limitations. Secondly, I had constant contact with the local laborers working there, who returned in the evenings or weekends to their homes in the nearby towns. This is how

I managed to be involved in supplying food. In most cases I managed to smuggle into camp the food that I had arranged. I could sell it and thus maintain the commercial cycle. When there were difficulties I suffered like the others. I was also dependant upon extra calories to survive.

The Polish civilians essentially craved things to wear: undergarments, coats and shoes were items in great demand, and we had a surplus of these in the camp. As a forced-laborer in the factory I could change clothes every day. And our brothers, who streamed in masses to the camps, were the ones who contributed these items, against their best interests– for our benefit.

And this is how it worked: each evening I went to the warehouse and exchanged my used clothing for new ones. The following morning the new clothing was passed to a Polish citizen, and he gave me his rags as a replacement, along with food items or money. That evening I returned to the clothing warehouse to exchange the Polish rags with the clothing of Jews who had arrived on the last transport – and trade them again... After a while the guards noticed that the exchanges at the warehouse happened too frequently. They decided to mark the clothing with the letters "KL" (*Konzentrationslager*, or concentration camp) and gave us shoes from two different pairs to make things difficult for us. And we still managed – we tried to locate the matching shoes throughout the living quarters, and we continued to trade the clothing despite the stamped letters.

During one of the clothing exchanges at the warehouse I received shoes with leather soles. The shoes that forced-laborers wore typically had wooden soles. Being an electrician who had to climb up ladders, I was entitled to leather-soled shoes, after presenting the proper authorization at the warehouse. The quality of the shoes that I received this time was so impressive that I decided not to trade them but to wear them myself.

After weeks of strenuous walking and hard work, as I sat on

a wooden bench in the shack, I noticed that a white cloth was poking out between the worn stitch-work of the sole. I was certain that a treasure was concealed within. I remember feeling my heart pounding strongly. Whoever had hidden the unidentified object in the bottom of the shoe had done an excellent job. All the shoes, and of course all the clothing, underwent the most thorough search before coming to us. Every stitch was opened, each double cloth was singled out, and every suspicious protrusion was cut open. Gold, silver and diamonds were frequently discovered in the lapels and soles. The chance that we prisoners would find something of value was very slim. And here was my shoe, with a piece of white cloth bulging out!

I waited for nightfall. With a pounding heart and trembling fingers I unraveled the sole and felt with my fingers, while under the blanket, the very edge of a cotton sack. My breathing faltered; perhaps even stopped. I slowly opened the sack and inside –my God – I felt several diamonds. It was a treasure. A real treasure. After calming down I asked myself: diamonds, but what can I do with them in a forced-labor camp? Who will take on the risk of dealing in diamonds? In addition I asked myself, perhaps they are fake, polished shards of glass? I concluded with myself that I had a problem. On the one hand I had diamonds in my possession, but on the other hand who will believe that they are real? A real problem, I told myself. I put the pouch in my coat pocket and could hardly sleep.

The next day we didn't go out to work, it was a sabbatical day. Even these days occurred in the factory. I wandered around the camp holding the sack tightly against me. I quickly came to the conclusion, that if I could replace the diamonds with something more tangible it would be easier for me to trade with the Poles. Here and there I whispered into ears that I knew and trusted that I had an unusual commodity in my pocket, perhaps someone was interested.

Towards evening a fellow from another block approached

me. I did not recognize him. "Moishe," he addressed me, "it has been rumored that you have diamonds."

"Who told you?" I asked. I wasn't afraid since he was a prisoner like me. It was true, that here and there informers were a threat, but they were rare. Not like in the ghetto.

"The rumor passed from mouth to ear", he said. "Don't be suspicious, I am like you".

"Yes, I have diamonds." I said.

"I'll give you a watch for diamonds," he said without hesitating. He didn't even offer to check the merchandise.

"A watch!" I said in amazement. A watch was a rare necessity. For a watch one could receive real luxury items. Bread, salami, cognac, cigarettes and more.

"You don't have to give me all the diamonds. I'll be satisfied with half of them." he offered.

I wasn't worried for a minute. He didn't even know how many diamonds I had and here he was, offering me a watch for half of them! Apparently he knew someone who was looking for diamonds and he would get a fortune from him.

I had nothing to do with the diamonds, and so I fetched the pouch that was buried in my shirt, counted out half the number of diamonds and placed them in his outstretched hand. He stared at them a few seconds, put his hand into his shirt pocket and gave me a watch. I felt that we had both profited. The fellow and the diamonds disappeared and I was left with a watch ticking inside my shirt.

The following morning, even before leaving for work, I was told that they were looking for me. "Me?" I asked the block leader.

"You!" he replied firmly, "They are already waiting for you at the gate."

I felt awful. It's called trembling knees. I ran to the bathroom and dumped diarrhea. For a moment I thought that I should dump the watch and diamonds. Just for a moment.

Maybe they can save me, I thought, and returned to the line.

I barely returned to the electrician's *commando* unit and advanced with it to the camp gate.

At the gate there were ridiculous ceremonies, and we were forced to listen to the daily marshal music played by the camp's orchestra.

"Prisoner number 127942 must stay in place." I heard what I had feared.

I was dumbstruck. The *commando* unit continued on its way. Some of the men managed to glance behind before they were screamed at for doing so.

Rakash, an S.S. man from the camp, ordered me to remain by the gate. I stood in place and stared at the disappearing *commando* group. Rakash approached me and stared at me with a piercing look.

"Where is the watch?" he demanded.

I didn't answer.

Rakash lifted his boot, stamped it on my foot and punched me fiercely: he didn't want me to fall.

"Where is the watch?" he asked again.

I took the watch out of my shirt and gave it to him.

"Why did you take the watch?" he screamed at me.

"I promised to give the equivalent to the one who gave me the watch", I answered. My lips were dry.

"What did you promise to give?", he shouted.

"A special belt." I answered. "A belt that can easily be made in the factory."

Rakash stared at the watch and placed it in his pants pocket.

"Run after your *commando* group!" he ordered.

I was so surprised by his behavior that I didn't wait for anything. I flew to my *commando* group as if the speed would keep my soul. I didn't want to give him a moment to change his mind.

I knew that the story had just begun. That day I couldn't work. I knew that the approaching evening would reveal my punishment.

"In the afternoon you must go to the prisoner's command post." One of the factory workers told me. I knew that the issue was not closed.

"Tell me how this all happened." the officer shouted at me.

I tried my best to describe what had happened, from the moment of finding the pouch in my shoe. I realized that he knew. Other prisoners already knew, so why shouldn't he know? I told myself that this time I would tell the truth. I had nothing to lose. I didn't want to be punished twice for the same incident.

"Who is the fellow who gave you the watch?" he asked.

"I don't know." I felt that he believed me. "Maybe I'll see him this evening at the camp." I added.

"When you return to camp this evening you must show up in my office!" he ordered me.

At the end of the work day we returned to the camp. I feared meeting Rakash at the gate. He wasn't there.

I immediately reported to the camp headquarters.

"Return to your block." he instructed me.

I didn't have the courage to ask him what happened.

"Rakash has been arrested on suspicion of doing business with prisoners." he said as I was leaving.

When I returned to the block the prisoners seemed surprised. Although no one said a word, they didn't believe that I had gotten off so easily.

Only later did I learn that Rakash had been associated with several prisoners who were involved in trading various luxury items. That morning he was caught in one of the blocks when he was intoxicated, as drunk as Lot (of the Bible), and placed under arrest by the Germans.

That night I also couldn't fall asleep.

Several days passed and nothing happened. Rakash had disappeared. The man that I traded with had disappeared. Suddenly, one morning, I saw Rakash at the gate post as we were standing in the staging area listening to the marshal music and waiting. I feared for my life. I wanted to stoop low so that he would not see me. I was sure that that he was still looking for me and the story was not finished. He hadn't said the final word, or dealt the last blow.

As our *commando* reached the gate, our Kapo announced: "*Commando* 27 electricians unit with 20 men leaving the camp."

"Electricians?" Rakash thundered. "Electricians?" he screamed again. "No way!" he barked.

"Black market dealers! Traders in watches, blankets and diamonds!" he shouted after several seconds. Then he looked at me and said in a loud voice: "You are lucky. If they hadn't arrested me, you would see those black diamonds" His meaning was that I would be sent to work in coal mining, work that was considered equivalent to a death sentence.

After a few days the true picture of my trading interlude emerged. The watch that was discovered on me had gone from hand to hand several times. After each rotation it returned to Rakash's faithful hands. This damned watch had slain many victims. Rakash had given it to a fellow with whom he traded liquor. The man would usually receive alcohol for the watch. He only had to inform Rakash who had the watch so that Rakash could retrieve the treasure that rolled into his hands, either on the way in or out of the camp.

The fate of the prisoner who dealt with Rakash was determined by the internal camp underground that indicted informers and ensured their punishment.

In this camp, the harshest punishment was imposed on a prisoner who returned from work without a coat. Whoever returned that way was suspected of doing business with civilians. A member of the underground swiped the coat belonging to Rakash's collaborator.

The last time that man was seen was by the gate, caught without a coat. We no longer feared him again.

The Food Chain

Little by little I became known as an organizer of food. So I wasn't surprised when one of the warehouse managers in camp made contact with me. "Can you get food for me?" he asked.

"What will you give me in exchange?"

"Clothing, and as much as you want." he answered. Clothing was useful and easy to barter. The task was very simple. In the evening I received an extra shirt from the stock-keeper, which I wore the next day on top of my shirt. At the factory, I removed it and gave it to one of the Poles, with whom I worked, and of course had business relations.

In one particular instance that I can describe, this Pole was a metal- worker and his workshop was in the basement of the building where I myself worked. During a week or more I delivered several shirts to the Pole, and he was supposed to bring me food, which I then gave to the stock-keeper.

"All the shirts that you gave me were stolen." the Pole informed me towards the end of the week. "Not even one shirt remained with me." he added.

I knew that this created a problem. The food chain was stuck. Someone in the chain would get screwed. I was worried that I was the one to be punished this time. It was obvious that the chain didn't end with the stock-keeper.

"All the shirts were stolen." I told the warehouse manager when I returned to camp that evening.

"I don't believe you," he raised his voice. "You're lying!" he said, with a trace of fear.

"I'm not lying." I stood my ground.

He paused for a moment and then said to me: "Tomorrow afternoon there is supposed to be an S.S. inspection at the workshop. When the German soldier approaches you" he added, "start speaking with the Polish metal-worker, even though this is forbidden. The German will know what to do."

I was amazed at his brazenness. He was instructing me to speak to a civilian during a German inspection? I was astonished. "You must know that it is forbidden to do this, and more so in front of the German!" I said, in an aggressive tone. But I had no other choice. I knew that the circle was still open.

The next day, in the afternoon, I went down to the workshop and made excuses for my arrival with a job I had to do. I avoided contact with the Polish metal-worker until I saw the S.S. man approaching.

"How are you doing?" I addressed the surprised civilian in Polish, so the German will hear but not understand. The Pole, who feared the German, started shouting loudly: "Give me the key!" He wanted the German to think we were talking about work. The German approached with quick steps and asked the Pole, "Why are you talking to a prisoner?" He seemed upset. "What is going on here?"

I didn't hesitate and said to the German: "I gave this man things and he took everything without giving anything in return." The German screamed at the Pole: "You do business with prisoners? If you don't return all that you have received from him by tomorrow morning, you will wear his clothes and he will wear yours. And you will take his place in the concentration camp!".

The Pole began to cry and said that he had four children and that the goods he had received had been stolen. This made no impression on the S.S. soldier as he left the basement.

The next day I got back most of the shirts, and instead of those missing - a full-bodied salami.

What was the relationship between the prominent stock-keepers and the Germans? I didn't think much about this question. Especially since I got back what had been stolen from me.

* * *

The arms factory operated 7 days a week, 365 days a year. The forced-laborers were given a rest once every two weeks, on Sunday. However, whoever wanted could go to the factory on that day. The supervision at the factory was more lax on Sundays while in the camp itself there were assemblies and officer reviews and the supervision was actually stricter. Since the Germans let each one decide for themselves, it wasn't unusual to go to work on Sunday. The exit to work, and the return back to camp, proceeded in perfect order like every other day of the week. But the supervision was somewhat superficial.

One day I received two packs of cigarettes and two packages of butter. I hid them in my toolbox. I knew that if I wanted to smuggle them into camp, Sunday would be the best. So, on the following Sunday I went to work along with many others. To tell the truth, I did not work that much; I wandered around the factory waiting until we returned to camp. I hid what I wanted to smuggle in my clothing and marched in the line.

But the laws of statistics didn't work this time. I had already noticed from a distance that the guards at the gate had been reinforced. The Germans, always unpredictable, searched us more carefully that day.

"Get out of line, outside!" one of the Germans shouted at me as I passed the gate.

I stood outside the procession. The same German performed

a quick search on me. He found the treasure – two packages of butter and two packs of cigarettes that were placed carefully at my feet.

Another S.S. soldier approached me. "Where did you get this?", he barked and pointed at the goods.

"I found it." I answered innocently, fearing the worst of all.

"Where?" he screamed, "Where did you find it?"

"In the factory, near the sewer pipes." I replied, trembling.

"I've already been guarding in the factory for two years and I never found anything." he raised his voice.

The soldier returned and recorded my number and my merchandise and went on to the next victim standing next to me. The S.S. man called to the *Lageuralteste* who was dressed in his white Sunday dress clothing. There was an upside down green triangle on his lapel signifying that he used to be a thief, and was brought from prison, like many others, to the concentration camp to be educated until his release.

"Were his identification details recorded?" the *Lageuralteste* asked the S.S. soldier.

"Affirmative ! Yes !", the S.S. soldier clicked his reply.

"You have luck, today's my birthday, so I won't beat you." The *Lageuralteste* said to me.

"Congratulations", I replied brazenly, "I hope that you are released soon".

Neither the *Lageuralteste* nor the S.S. man had noticed that my identification number was written on the side of one of the cigarette packs that I had brought. Before I managed to leave the gate the pack was torn apart and its contents were distributed among the prison guards in the area.

Even today, when I notice someone writing details on a cigarette pack, I know that he doesn't intend to remember them for long. A cigarette pack has a certain future – within a short time it gets emptied of its contents and tossed away.

When the *blockaltesta* of my living quarters heard the story he called me over and said: "Idiot, you should have told the S.S. man that the cigarettes and butter were for me!"

Really? It seems that was the last thing I needed.

Despite this, I couldn't fall asleep for two weeks.

* * *

"Were there prostitutes in the factory?" I asked my father. "Why do you ask?" my father answered with a question, as usual. "Because I assume that there must have been sexual activity in the factory." I answered. "I'll tell you something that I've never told anyone before." Dad appeared to be sweetening a secret.

* * *

There was forbidden sexual activity going on in the huge factory. Women – local Poles, and perhaps women prisoners – worked at many jobs in the factory. They were also hungry. And they also wanted to get what they could outside the law. This could be done by indulging in the world's oldest profession. And what didn't they do to get more? How does a brothel work? How do you accomplish this in a factory supervised from every angle by Germans?

For every *commando* (or collection of groups) there was a shack in the factory, where the person in charge stayed during working hours. We received our daily meals in the shack. Each day, at the beginning, we arrived at the shack and from there we also returned to the camp at the end of the workday. The same shack was a kind of information center for the *commando*. After a while certain group leaders converted these shacks into brothels. That's a fact.

One of the local girls, who knew the Kapo and was ready to fulfill the extended role, would enter the shack. Whoever wanted to enjoy her services would give the Kapo 20 marks. Fifty percent of the prostitute's fee would remain in his hands and 50 percent was the woman's take. This would yield a tidy profit.

The Kapo was responsible for all of his group's activities. And let's remember that some of them were pimps before the war. The Germans utilized thieves, minor criminals, and pimps as authorities. It was as simple as that.

* * *

"And here's something spicy." Dad said.

* * *

On one particular Sunday, when we were not forced to go to work unless it was desired, some of the *Commando* 9 men went out to the factory; they were among the elite prisoners of the camp. They assumed that the supervision would be more lax than usual that day, so they could indulge the prostitutes in the shack. But rumors about the "corruption" reached the Germans who raided the shack during these activities. The punishment was light this time – breaking the hands and feet of all those involved. Whoever appeared wounded in the days that followed was suspected of receiving his due for partying with a prostitute.

* * *

During the war, in September of 1939, a piece of shrapnel pierced the palm of my hand. It was painful for several days and then I forgot about it. The difficult work at Buna – by then I worked as a certified electrician – caused much pressure on the shrapnel and it began to show signs of life. The palm of my left hand swelled, and although I attempted to conceal it,

I couldn't use my hand. The high temperature caused by my hand's infection forced me to go to the infirmary.

I waited outside the infirmary. I knew that if my temperature didn't exceed 38 degrees, I didn't have a chance to see the doctor; even 37.5 wasn't enough to qualify for a doctor.

"Look", I turned to the Polish male-nurse who worked there and pointed to my palm. He looked at it and agreed to get me in to see the Polish doctor, who was from Krakow.

"When did this happen?" the doctor asked. So I told him. He didn't seem to believe that so much time had passed since the injury. Despite this he continued to grasp the palm of my hand: "Write a note allowing him to go to the infirmary tomorrow", the doctor told the nurse, "He must have an operation." he added. Later on I gave the note to the *blockaltesta*.

The following day was beautiful. The sun was shining and the sky was blue. I remember it as if it was today. I arrived at the infirmary. More precisely, it was the regional hospital. While still standing outside I was asked to remove all my clothing, and I stood naked in the line, together with other prisoners. Everyone waited to go in for an operation. I stood there several hours after which I was led respectfully into the operating room. In the operating room I was requested to lie down on a bed, which was surrounded by three male-nurses dressed in white. One of them placed a towel with ether on my face. I remember counting to nine and falling asleep.

When they woke me I asked the nurse: "Why did you wake me?", and he answered me with a sharp slap on my face.

The hospital at Buna was relatively large. There were 10,000 prisoners in camp, and those who became ill were admitted for treatment there. Some of those admitted had undergone operations like mine, or operations for broken bones or appendicitis. Whoever survived the operation was entitled to stay up to two weeks recovering in the hospital block. With the aid of money or food it was possible to gain another week to recuperate. Immediately afterwards the prisoners returned to work.

There was of course a *selectzia* in the camp. The commandant instigated this, and it was obvious that whoever failed was sent to the gas chamber.

* * *

They covered the cut with toilet paper. I was granted six days of sick leave – six full days without going out to work! Since I wasn't confined to a bed, I could circulate in the camp at will. These excursions during the work-day, when the camp was almost empty, took me to places I did not know existed.

On one of these rest days I reached an area that was relatively far away from my block. I saw that the area was fenced in, although it was inside the camp, among the residence shacks. Beyond the fence I saw a swimming pool and several women in bathing suits sat alongside it. A surrealistic image in true form.

In the past, I had heard hints of the existence of the oldest profession in the camp. But I had never been exposed to it nor did I speak to anyone involved. Now I believed that I had arrived at the place. I leaned on the fence and approached one of the girls closest to me: "Why do you do it?", I asked.

"Do you want bread?" was her answer.

"I would be happy to receive some." I replied.

Perhaps I didn't understand her philosophical answer. I didn't get any bread because they had none.

I continued to stare and asked: "Are you here of your own will or did they force you?"

"By force." she said. "They forced me".

Her friend, who until that moment totally ignored me, threw my way: "They took *you* by force – you old whore?" and she added with a sneer, "You came here willingly."

There were prisoners who were entitled to this escort service, non-Jews of course. They paid from the premiums they received from the factory. Yes, we received money for our work. We used the money at the internal canteen to buy toothpaste or various brushes. The Germans signed for the work in units of time. Whoever worked more quickly received local currency – premium fees – for use in the canteen. I never went to the canteen, I always converted the money into calories.

A non-Jewish prisoner who wanted escort services, and had about 20 marks from the camp, could legally sign up. He received a date that suited everyone. When his turn came, he got a pass for the prostitute's shack. The shack was long and had many rooms. In each there was a woman.

After a doctor's exam the room to which the prisoner was assigned was cast by lottery. When the bell was sounded the prisoner entered the room and remained there for a measured duration of sex. Another ring of the bell signaled the end of activities. Then the whole process repeated itself.

Interesting, efficient, German, was it not?

* * *

The engineer who was responsible for Buna was a political prisoner named Patzel. He didn't imagine the real reason that I was there. He was certain that I was a political prisoner like him.

"What did you say to make them put you into prison?" he asked when I began to work with him.

I answered by raising my hand and pointing to the number on my arm. He stared at the number and was sure that I hadn't understood him. He repeated the question slowly. And I responded by stretching my left arm past his face to show the truth.

"What's that?" he asked.

"A number", I replied.

"Who did that to you?"

"The Germans."

"Why?"

"Because I am a Jew."

Silence.

I requested that he turn his eyes south in the direction of Birkenau and said to him: "Do you see the smoke on the horizon? Do you know what that is?"

"No."

I explained it to him.

The engineer took a handkerchief out of his coat pocket and began to dry his tears. Had he really not known?

* * *

One day I was asked to connect a temporary telephone exchange to a permanent exchange and the electrical grid. I prepared all the relevant materials for the transfer so that the phone system would be disconnected the least amount of time possible. The engineer Patzel, being responsible for the project, gave me the appropriate instructions. When I completed all the preparations, I approached the chief telephone operator and informed her that I would disconnect the exchange for several minutes in order to perform the transfer. I returned to the workplace and began the task.

A few minutes later, while I was absorbed in the work, the factory manager arrived on a motorcycle.

"Who gave you permission to disconnect the phone exchange?", he screamed at me.

"This is an order from the engineer responsible for the project, and I coordinated it with the head operator." I answered bluntly.

"Follow me to the basement." the manager shouted.

We entered the building. When we had just entered the hall,

by the doorway, he hit me on the head. I realized that I would not leave the basement alive. Deciding to take advantage of the excessive weight and slowness of the man, I hastened my steps and escaped to the shack of our *commando*, and explained what had happened to both the Kapo and work foreman who were there. The foreman recorded the story as I reported it to him, and later on he complained to the S.S. man about the incident.

Remember that the factory had stiff rules regarding worker and employer relations. It was absolutely forbidden for a civilian to hit a prisoner. Afterwards I learned that the manager of the factory tried to use the telephone when he discovered that the exchange was disconnected. The operator and project manager had neglected to tell him about the planned disruption. He called the operator on the red line, which does not pass through the phone exchange, and she informed him that one of the prisoners announced the exchange would be disconnected. He began to go wild and consequently I found myself before him.

A few days later I was informed that because of the Kapo's complaint that the factory manager whipped me there would be a trial. "What do I need a trial for?" I asked the foreman, and afterward Patzel.

"These are the rules here." Patzel answered. And to encourage me said: "I'll come to the trial and defend you. I am responsible for what happened. You're a good worker." he added.

The trial took place in one of the open spaces within the factory. When I arrived at the "court yard" I saw the judge, the accused, the prosecutor and several other people who arrived in the yard. However, the central witness for the defense, the engineer Patzel, had disappeared as if the earth had swallowed him. My eyes searched everywhere for him. He wasn't there.

The judge was the S.S. man Rakash, and he had brought two more S.S. men for reinforcement. The foreman who presented the complaint stood by my side. The Kapo did not come. The factory manager was also there. Fatter than ever, relaxed, sure of himself. I felt disgusted, but more than anything I remember that the pounding of my heart could have been heard from a distance.

We stood in a circle. It's difficult to describe my feelings when Rakash came closer to the foreman and me, as we stood side by side. He raised his voice, looked at me, and screamed: "He didn't kill you!" He paused a moment and then added the question: "What are you complaining about?"

Was I supposed to answer? In fact I didn't get the opportunity.

Rakash turned quickly and kicked me once, and added a kick to the foreman too. He told us to disappear.

The trial was over. Justice had been done. I remained alive.

Immediately after the trial I returned to my workplace where I met the engineer who hadn't come. "Why didn't you come to the trial?" I asked, "You promised, after all".

"You already know why by yourself." he said, and did not elaborate.

The next morning I arrived at work as usual. The burden of the trial was lifted from me. But I didn't know how the factory manager would react when he saw me. I was, after all, a prisoner without rights, whose life was worth less than a garlic peel, who had disrupted his daily routine and made him appear at the trial as the accused. While I was trying to imagine what his reaction would be, I heard his motorcycle approaching the building. When he saw me he tipped his head towards me and said "Good morning." as if nothing had happened.

* * *

On Sundays there were several sports activities at Buna that distracted us from our dismal situation for a while. Soccer games or boxing were the main entertainment which we enjoyed in our free time – playing or watching. I even remember one time that there was a championship playoff among three football groups: prisoners, Germans, and Poles (cooks). Unbelievable. If I'm not mistaken, there was at least one man who had played in the past for the "Hakoach" (means "the strength" in Hebrew) team in Vienna, a recognized club at the time. The head referee for the game was the conductor of the Krakow orchestra, a Jew.

The Jews were better than the Germans and were on the verge of winning. The referee feared a victory by his people, and towards the end called for a penalty kick from the eleventh meter in favor of the Germans. The camp commander who watched the game saw that the judgment was wrong. He halted the match, kicked out the Jewish referee, and began refereeing himself. The penalty was obviously canceled. In this championship the Jews beat the Germans, but were then beaten by the Poles.

Jews beating Germans? Is this possible? More than that, who can believe that one can work so hard, to live in a state of malnutrition and also play soccer? Apparently whoever played soccer was entitled to work in the kitchen, in the warehouse, or in offices, so that food was not lacking. One of my friends, Moishele Grinbaum[17], who was a football player in Mezritch, refused to play in Buna. I told him that it was worth his while to play, because then he could get better work, but he continued to refuse.

One Sunday a boxing match was organized between two professionals – a boy from Saloniki called Jacko and a French lad who answered, if I'm not mistaken, to the name Bernard. We, the prisoners, stood around the spectator's perimeter. The fight was brief. The Frenchman had the upper hand. He was stronger and more experienced and he knocked the Greek down within several minutes. Immediately afterwards, one could see that he was also shaken up by the beating. He approached

---

17. Moishele Grinbaum survived the war and died only a few years ago in the United States.

the Greek, lifted him, hugged him and whispered in his ear (so they say): "We are brothers, I don't want to kill you, that's not my intention".

About a year later I saw the Greek in Brussels. A circus appeared in one of the main boulevards. In the clearing before the central tent two boxers from the circus were battling. After their show they turned to the audience and asked if anyone was willing to fight one of the boxers. Suddenly Jacko, the guy from Saloniki whom I saw at Buna, rolled up his sleeves and waited for his opportunity. This time he was victorious.

* * *

There was also an orchestra in Buna that had two roles: to give us pleasure on Sundays, and every day, near the gate, to play marching sounds that eased the task of counting prisoners as they entered and left the camp. Perhaps they also played for the Germans on special occasions.

Humanism

The bombing of the Buna work-camp began in 1944. The Allies realized that the huge factory where I worked was serving the German war effort. They knew that in Buna, for example, they produced oil from coal so they began bombing it continuously. As a result, the Germans decided to reinforce the main building, and accelerated building its cement enclosure on all sides. The number of workers increased with every day. We were sure the building was important and was a strategic target. The bombings were so accurate that the number of German casualties grew tremendously.

The bombings prompted the German soldiers serving in the watch towers to demand from their officers that the exposed area surrounding the towers also be reinforced. The task of reinforcing the towers was assigned to a group of Jewish prisoners. Alongside each watchtower the Germans built an underground bunker. The idea was that if the alarm of an impending bombing attack was sounded, the guards would descend from the towers near the fence to the bunkers. When the all-clear was sounded they would return to their stations. Each bunker was supposed to house two soldiers. A stairway led to a small space that was three meters deep.

Due to the proximity of the bunkers to the fence, one group of prisoners came up with an idea, to continue digging past the fence, so that there would be a secure underground passage to freedom. The group invested enormous energy in the implementation of their plan, and they managed to dig a trench that started at the bunker and ended just beyond the fence. Only three people were aware of this secret trench-digging project.

One day a spotlight had burned out as it hung from a tower near the fence and bunker where the trench sprang forth. The

German maintenance crew arrived at the location. One of the soldiers climbed a ladder and changed the bulb. When he finished the job, he began to climb back down the ladder. Suddenly he rotated and turned to his colleagues, who restlessly milled around below him. He attempted to outsmart them and rose instead of descending, and jumped from the ladder to the gravel-covered ground. His landing sounded strange. Instead of the noise expected when landing upon gravel, the sound of impact had a certain resonance to it, which caused the group of German soldiers to look amazed.

The officer in charge screamed something in German. The soldiers began to clear away the gravel and discovered the wooden beams that hid the opening to the trench.

When we returned from work that day we already knew that the three prisoners who were among those who built the bunker were yanked from wherever they had been working and were sent to jail following an investigation.

Typically, when there were special events like this in the camp, the Germans would assemble us in the spacious parade grounds. The camp commanders stood on the platform and one of them would remind us of our position there and what we could expect if and when we violated their rules. This time they skipped the public exhibition. The event passed without any exception to the daily procedures and assemblies at the work camp. But the rumor about the attempted escape and the three "heroes" went through the camp like a brushfire. There was a kind of group pride among the prisoners that someone had dared to break the rules and had almost succeeded.

* * *

About a month after the trench incident, as we were returning from work, we were again directed to the assembly field. The three poles that were set up behind the platform hinted about what was to happen.

Only when the last prisoner had stood in the field, before darkness fell, did we see the three accused dressed in sacks being led by S.S. men. We couldn't see their hands.

An S.S. officer read their crimes and punishment. The Germans allowed them to give speeches before the enormous audience they had assembled there. At night I can still hear their final words.

One of the accused said that he hoped that they were the last to be punished in this miserable war. The second said that he hoped that we prisoners would witness the hanging of his hangmen. And the third had thanked the Germans for transferring his brother to another camp so that he wouldn't observe his hanging.

Real humanism.

* * *

One day in 1944 a siren was heard throughout the factory. The British, who were aware of the strategic importance of the factory and wanted to destroy it, were accustomed to sending over scores of bombers from time to time that tried to damage the fortified building.

Besides my regular work as an electrician, I received an emergency assignment: operating the main generator that was inside management's fortified bunker. So I enjoyed the privilege of staying in that bunker during the bombings.

"What are you doing here?" I heard the scream of an S.S. man who was also inside the shelter.

"Operating the generator." I answered innocently.

"Out with you!" he ordered with a shrill voice.

"It is forbidden to be outside the buildings during an air-raid." I replied. "Whoever is found outside the buildings when the sirens alarm, gets shot."

"Get out of here and go to the next building and I'll stand at the opening and supervise you." he reprimanded me.

I went upstairs and the German followed me. I left the building. About 20 meters separated between the building I had been in and the one I was supposed to reach.

The German could easily have injured me, as could someone from above. After a short and crazy run I found myself inside an abandoned building. Its workers preferred to stay in the management building that was more protected.

After a few minutes I caught my breath again, then sat on the floor and lit a cigarette. Through the smoke cloud of the first drag I saw someone enter the space, although it was not protected. I felt that they were looking for me. First they kick me out of the most defended bunker in the area, and afterwards, when I sit down, out jumps a German from nowhere and grabs me 'with my pants down'.

"Come here." he said.

I put the cigarette out with my foot and approached him.

"Do you know that it is forbidden to smoke in a bunker?" he asked.

"Yes", I said.

"Give me your particulars". He recorded the number tattooed on my arm and left. I knew that I would be punished.

At the end of that week, during the daily assembly, the number 127942 was called out. I was ordered to remain standing where I was after the procession. When all the other prisoners had left, a few prisoners remained standing in place and waiting for their trial.

Suddenly the camp commander appeared opposite me and shouted in my ear the following sentence: "127942 you do not smoke cigarettes!"

I was amazed. The German continued on his way, passed the

next prisoner and shouted at him a sentence I could not catch, and that is what he did until he passed the last prisoner who had remained in place.

Why did he say that sentence to me? What was I supposed to do? I actually did smoke, so why did he tell me that I didn't smoke? I reviewed the sentence several times in an attempt to understand it, and I didn't notice that three S.S. men, and among them the despicable Rakash, were closing in on me. One of the three fixed his gaze on me and growled me: "On this and that day you were caught in a bunker, during an air-raid alert, and you were smoking!"

The only sentence I could utter, as if spitting out some mantra that I had learned by heart, was: "I don't smoke cigarettes". I repeated loudly what the camp commander had said.

Rakash looked at me and said: "Get out of here, disappear!"

I'll never understand what motivated the camp commander to pass by me and dictate what I should say a few moments later, and be saved.

* * *

I don't know the Buna Camp commander's role in the reduction of the Jewish population. I know that he had some favorable points worth recalling:

He was the one who had told me before my trial "you don't smoke", and thus I had escaped without punishment.

He insisted that a punishment be administered according to the schedule. For example, if someone was sentenced to harsh work for one month, he made sure that the work ceased on time and was replaced by something else.

He gave the order that during rain and snow hats need not be removed when passing through the gate upon leaving or entering the camp.

They told the story about him approaching one of the prisoners on a particularly cold day to inquire why he wasn't wearing a sweater and coat. The prisoner answered that he had just been released from the hospital, and he was on the way to his shack. The officer requested that the prisoner accompany him back to the hospital.

"Are you the doctor who released this prisoner?" he asked the doctor whom the prisoner pointed to.

"Yes, why?", the doctor inquired.

"In that case, give him your sweater and coat. This is not how you release prisoners."

And that is how it happened. The prisoner left in the direction of his block outfitted with the doctor's sweater and coat – orders were to be obeyed.

They say that he searched for former Buna prisoners in Buchenwald. Why?

The Journey to Buchenwald

The entire night of January 15th, 1945 we heard the crash and thunder of immense destruction wrought by bombs. We knew that the factory was being targeted by the Allies. During the bombings it was absolutely forbidden to leave the blocks. Obviously there were no bunkers for us to hide within. There were no sirens either. We heard the planes and the sound of explosions. We also clearly heard the sounds of German cannons firing against the planes. Some of the bombs, not many, fell in the vicinity of the camp where we stayed. There were prisoners who took advantage of the breached camp fence that was hit and collapsed. I only heard this after liberation.

The following morning, the 16th of January, there was no wakeup as a prelude to leaving for work. Afterwards we were told that the guards who were supposed to accompany us to work were guarding the camp itself, and there wasn't sufficient manpower.

Nonetheless, by 8 AM they got us organized and we finally walked to the factory. There we were ordered to busy ourselves with repairs and work related to cleaning the area from the bombing damage. The factory didn't look the same from day to day. The British work wasn't bad. We cleared the roads and removed destroyed buildings.

That day there was a sense of losing control. The prisoners began to talk about hiding in the factory and not returning to the camp. Nobody had ever dared mentioning that before. Apparently there were those who hid and in fact didn't return to Buna. It could be that I made a mistake by not hiding, since the Russians liberated the factory grounds about 10 days after we left the place, and the thunder of their cannons could already be heard in the camp.

"Work in the factory has ceased", the guards told us towards evening on our way back to camp. That morning they still counted us upon exiting as usual, but on our return the headcount was abandoned. We felt the current chaos in sharp contrast to the absolute order that had prevailed in the camp until then.

Soldiers standing at the entrance to the camp diverted us to the clothing warehouses where we received blankets. Remember that this was the middle of January and the European winter was at its peak. Past the fences we saw transports of people traveling on the roads. After we received blankets we returned to the shacks. Towards dark they assembled us and gave each one a ration of bread (about 120 grams). We brought the blankets to this meeting, as ordered. We began walking late at night. I estimate that approximately 10,000 men began the march. Surrounding us I saw many S.S. soldiers with rifles and several with machine guns. Today I know that we walked in the direction of Gleiwitz, but then, who among us knew where we were going? Who even recognized the place?

We marched the whole night in a long procession. Towards morning we arrived in an area that included a huge factory for red bricks. We were led into the enormous factory with straw spread on the floor. Actually, it was quite possible to escape from the transport. It was possible to hide, and I assume that a group of prisoners did. Most of the guards were older Hungarian S.S. men, and it appeared that they didn't quite understand their roles in this march. There were instances when the prisoners carried the weapons for the tired prison guards. I don't know if in fact there was an organized escape from the place. Perhap there was?

My friend Gad Finkelshtein told me that he had escaped from the his transport several weeks afterwards in the area of the brick factory, and other prisoners who I later met in Israel said, that when our procession left the factory, some of them remained behind and covered themselves with straw. German soldiers who arrived later found and killed them.

We arrived at Gleiwitz the following night. The temperature was 20 degrees below zero. On the way there I could no longer walk with the blanket that protected me from the cold and I discarded it. In Gleiwitz we were placed inside an abandoned women's camp. Each one received a platform on which he could rest. Basically they forced 200 men into a hall that could only occupy 40 people. Despite the cold outside, the hall began to heat up from our bodies. The Germans, and the non-Jewish prisoners who watched over us, began pushing people outside while shouting "Jews out", so that the room temperature would drop. I recall that my body burned from heat, my face was glowing and my palms were red. The solution was to be covered with snow. During the night I entered and left the shack many times. When I felt the intense cold I returned and was squashed into the space of the shack, and when I heated up I left and laid myself down on the snow outside the block and attempted to fall asleep. And then I repeated the process again.

The next morning we were told that our convoy was being transferred to Austria. We were divided into groups so as not to climb onto the train all at once.

After the war I heard from several prisoners that the men of *Commando 9*, who were considered the elite group at the Buna camp, were murdered by their superiors in the forest nearby the women's camp.

From the camp we walked in the direction of the railroad

train. There we climbed up onto open railcars, with snow falling upon most of time. We sat on the floor of the cars and traveled for about four days. At first we apparently traveled towards Austria, but the direction changed along the way. I am certain that we traveled through Czechoslovakia, but I don't remember the exact route we took. Finally we arrived at Buchenwald. The snow served us as food and water, but many died on the way from the cold and hunger.

* * *

"And what do you think was the worst of all during the trip?" Dad asked me and answered, "When we passed under the bridges".

* * *

Farmers stood on the bridges. They understood that we were suffering from the cold and hunger and they threw food leftovers at us. And at these moments the animal within mankind broke out. During the chase after a few calories violent fights broke out among the prisoners, and several lost their lives there. The food that was swiped from hand to hand disintegrated and disappeared. We didn't see food but we did see animals. Once again, man was willing to kill his brother just to survive.

The war pushed man into terrible dilemmas. Humankind essentially disappeared and the inhuman character was revealed. If children could expose their parent's hiding place and vice versa, if brothers were prepared to kill their family members, why should we complain about a struggle for basic nourishment? The Germans brought out these terrible qualities in us because of our suffering, when in fact they acted like animals without enduring any suffering themselves.

We arrived at Buchenwald. Due to weakness caused by my hunger and being cold I could not descend from the boxcar. Local prisoners came to the car and helped me and others like me to get down. We slowly walked into the camp, where they undressed us. A barber shaved all the hair from my body, and I was placed into a barrel of disinfectant. My head was forced in because I didn't want to drown.

Only there, in the barrel, did I lose my grip on my brother Zeev's identification booklet and picture that I had found in Maidanek and guarded so carefully throughout this damned journey.

On the way to the shacks we received prisoner's clothing. I remember the taste of the first food that we received – a mixture of warm water in which potatoes had been cooked. I recall very well that feeling of the "hot" food passing through my gullet. The wounds of heartburn that I suffered can be felt even today.

They housed us in the shack upon wide platform boards, with about 15 people stuffed onto each board. We laid there like sardines in a can. One man's head touched his neighbor's feet. When one wanted to turn around, the whole group had to respond with a similar motion.

The next morning we were evacuated from the boards, lest we exhale our souls (die) within the shacks. We didn't work. We milled around near the shack and tried to warm up a bit in the sun. After several hours we discovered a water source and we washed ourselves.

Buchenwald was a camp for political prisoners. Nearby the camp the Germans assembled the V1 and V2 rockets. I know that the chairman of the German communist party, Thalmann was his name, was a prisoner in Buchenwald. He worked manufacturing missiles, and I was told that he was killed in one of the bombings on the place.

Picture 15 men lying on each of the boards. When food was distributed, the closest to the passage-way among the 15 prisoners received the rations for all those lying on the platform. In order to receive a full ration, we left the dead lying on the board and received food for them as well. But the first in line, who was usually strong and not necessarily a Jew, kept the rations of the dead for himself.

Since it was winter, and cold, the stench of the dead didn't rise up for a few days. And then, when the smell was already unbearable, we took them out of the shacks so that we could distinguish between the living and the dead.

I remember that I saw one of the prisoners detect that someone was still alive who already couldn't leave the shack. He hit him and forced him to die in order to steal his gold teeth. I recalled the fate of my own gold bridge.

* * *

The life in Buchenwald, like Maidanek, was unbearable. One morning they looked for 1,000 skilled workers for jobs. I gave my name and number to the man who was recording. In fact the next morning they called me to work. My friend Simon Fleishbein was also recorded, but he wasn't called. I remember the sad look in his eyes when he realized he was being separated from me. Due to the five year age difference, I felt responsible for him and I regretted the separation.

In the morning we left in a transport. Each of us got a slice of bread and we climbed up onto a train of closed boxcars. We sat on the floor of the car. S.S. soldiers stood by the doors and watched over us. Approximately ten minutes into the trip the train was bombed by British Spitfire planes. Apparently, they saw the Gestapo at the doorways and assumed that this was a military convoy. The planes flew over the train three times and bombed it. The train slowed down.

One of the prisoners near me wanted to see what was happening outside the boxcar and pushed me away from the crack through which I could see outside. At that instant he was killed, apparently by gunfire coming from one of the escort planes covering the bombers. He fell upon me and his blood streamed onto my clothes. Whoever saw me immediately concluded that I had been wounded because of my blood-soaked jacket.

During the third bombing wave the train got stuck and stopped and we jumped from the cars. Many were injured and killed. I estimated that 400 people were killed, most of them prisoners.

When the planes disappeared, we lowered the dead and wounded from the boxcars. A train marked with the red cross arrived and evacuated the wounded. Injured prisoners were evacuated by the train, not just the German soldiers. Trucks that arrived afterwards took us to the camp in Sviberg'e. We reached this camp and they put us into a shack. There were no boards within. Everyone received a blanket and we lied down on straw that was spread upon the ground.

Sviberg'e

The following morning they arranged a march to reach the camp that was located within a forest. I saw people hanged during the war. They were all dead. But in Sviberg'e (Zwieberge) I saw for the first time people who were hanging alive while their heads were pointed downward. Similarly I saw other people who were tied to trees like dogs with a leash tied to their necks. All of this wordlessly explained to us the punishments issued for disobeying orders in this camp.

There were also Russian prisoners of war who sold cooked meat every evening. Later it was disclosed that this was human meat.

The introductory march ended without words.

I was assigned to work in laying iron rails. Others told me that this was harder work than it seemed. So when they then looked for men to work in the mines I signed up. There was also an option not to go out and work. But I was not prepared, nor were many others, to remain in the camp and fall prey to the abuse of the Russian POWs and the Ukrainians located there, who not only beat the Jews but also extorted their food rations from them.

To my misfortune, I was not chosen for the work detail in the mines.

* * *

The task of laying iron rails was the most difficult work that I had encountered in my whole life. If before this I had thought that digging up mortar, what I did in Buna, was hard work, then the laying of iron rails was several times more difficult. Many people died doing this job. I recall that we often left for work as a force of 100 people and only 50 returned on their legs. The sound of shouts that directed us to lift and transfer together the heavy steel beams – "Hey-Rik, Hey-Rik, Hey-Rik" – still resounds in my ears.

After two days at this difficult task I noticed that they were looking for 12 men for another job. They didn't say why. Everyone wanted to escape from laying the iron rails so the competition was fierce. I knew that I had no chance. The Germans encircled about 12 men and the others began to push and pull people from the circle in order to replace them. The Ukrainians, who were the strongest in the camp, were the ones who started the riot.

I stood on the sidelines with other prisoners. From within the commotion there suddenly appeared approximately ten S.S. soldiers who encircled the area where we were standing, and they dragged us outside the camp grounds.

"You are going to work." they told us. And so we began to march. We passed about five kilometers and we reached an area with mine excavations that had to be sealed with cement. Our job was to prepare the cement and to pour it into the mines until they were filled. Those responsible were German civilians, and to my relief these Germans were relatively decent to us personally. They even brought us leftover food, such as potato peels and bread.

The work was not as difficult as the iron rails, and the amount of food we received from the civilians was reasonable. I suppose that this saved me and the others from becoming nonentities (pathetic beings, or "nebbishim" in Yiddish).

The civilians only worked eight hours, so that we could have returned to camp in the afternoon. But the S.S. soldiers who guarded us could only bring us back at the end of the 12-hour work day, as was the schedule for the other prisoners, so every day we did odd jobs to finish the four hour quota.

The British continued to bomb this area as well. During the bombings we told our guards that entering the mine shafts was not safe, since they could be closed off if directly hit. At first they heeded our recommendation and we remained in the open space, but when they felt the machine-gun bullets shrieking past them, they decided to run to the mines and risk the entrance collapsing.

A month came and passed. Because of the comfortable work among the civilians and the reasonable amount of food, I was sorry that this job was finished.

* * *

When the work at the mines was done I returned to Sviberg'e. I worried about returning to the laying of iron rails, and I also did not want to remain in the camp because of the beatings from the Russians or the others who watched over us.

In camp it was forbidden to keep a plate on the boards. One day, when I was in the shack, the *blockaltesta* approached me. He was upset: "Why are you hiding a plate in the straw?" he asked me and pointed at a plate.

"I don't know what you are talking about", I replied.

"Then who does it belong to?" he boomed and swiped it from my board under the blanket.

"It's not mine", I answered adamantly. "I am not hiding any plate and I don't know who did this," and I added, "Maybe somebody hid it in my place so that I would be punished instead of him."

The answer did not satisfy him. The *blockaltesta* raised his arms and pummeled me with murderous blows. Part of the sensitivity that I still feel in my ribs until today came from those strikes. When I was released I looked for him. I wanted to get revenge, but when I recovered my life – I forgot about it.

* * *

"Can you arrange for me to work in the mines?" I requested of Moshe-Hirsch Eidelbaum, a foreman in one of the mines who came from Mezritch.

"I'll try, but I will have to give someone something in return", he replied.

I didn't really care who this "someone" was, even if it was he himself. That same evening I gave him my portion of bread.

"Tomorrow you will join me." he said after a few hours.

So I began to work digging tunnels in Herman Goering's factories. I assume that these mines were to serve as defensive basements against the atomic bomb. The same bomb that the Americans had.

The excavation work was very difficult. True, not as hard as laying iron rails but hard enough.

The work was varied. I worked at drilling the holes, planting explosives, stretching electrical wires, checking them and passing electricity for the ignition, and afterwards clearing the area of debris, strengthening the ceiling, and on to the next drilling. Holding the heavy drill above your head while doing the other tasks was the most difficult. Apparently the work foreman noticed that my contribution to the group was significant, so he occasionally brought me potato pancakes.

Many people died from this work as well. Whoever was injured was put to death later in the camp. One day I was also injured. A stone fell on my head and struck a powerful blow. A German medic arrived and bandaged me.

"At camp you must enter the infirmary", said the medic.

"Don't go to the infirmary." I heard him say after half an hour.

He also knew that the deadly injection that patients received there cured all illnesses.

* * *

The number of dead in the camp was huge. The Germans concentrated the bodies someplace, and on Sunday the living dealt with burying the dead. We dragged the bodies to an enormous brother's grave that was covered with trees, placed them in the pit, and the Germans poured in disinfectant and dirt.

One weekday we were ordered not to go to work. Canons could be heard in the distance. The officer said that since the number of dead was increasing, he wanted us to remain in the camp and clean it. When we finish cleaning we would go out to work.

The officer asked that his instructions would be translated into various languages. One of the translators, who was Czech, said while translating: "Of course you know the real reason that we are not going out to work." The German officer, who understood Czechoslovakian, asked the translator to actually repeat in a loud voice the inaccurate translation, and added that anybody who thinks otherwise is an idiot.

Obviously we didn't go out to work anymore. I remember well that on that day we received an extra portion of soup for some reason.

The March of Death

In the evening we got organized for what would later be called "The March of Death". All the prisoners were roused from their shacks, and the sick were placed on the floor.

"Anyone who cannot march knows very well the fate in store for them." the announcement blared in German over loudspeakers.

My friend Menachem Averbuch was sick and could not walk. I parted from him. He remained on one of the stretchers. Later on I discovered that they transported the sick westward in trucks.

Several of the prisoners hid within the camp and, although it was bombed that night, some survived.

We began to move that night. We walked several days towards the north. During the day we rested in the fields. We didn't receive water. Each of us got a spoonful of grain crumbs. I recall that one day a farmer's wagon carrying carrots passed by the transport. The hungry prisoners pounced on the wagon. The Germans began to shoot at the prisoners and killed some of them. Nobody cared, and nothing remained on the wagon except the bodies of several hungry prisoners.

During one of the stopovers I discovered radish roots in a field. I was so hungry that I began to eat it immediately and got heartburn from this herbal food. I had nothing to wash it down. My saliva had dried up and so I felt that bitterness for many hours.

Often the nights were white because the British dropped flare bombs in the area and one could see clearly for quite a distance. The colors of the night together with the artificial light in the beginning of spring were unforgettable. Every day many fell on the way and the convoy shrank considerably.

* * *

"We'll escape", I said to Moshe-Hirsch on the fifth or sixth night of the march. That evening I felt especially weak.

"I have a blanket the same color as the pavement. I'll start walking slowly to remain at the end of the convoy. And then I shall fall. Whatever will be, will be." I added.

And that is actually what I did. I started to slow down, and after a while I found myself at the end of the line. I fell upon the road and covered myself. Here and there I heard the voices of marchers. I assumed that they were the rearguard of our transport.

I waited a few more minutes and then I heard the sound of boot-nails on the road. I didn't move. I knew that S.S. men were marching at the end of the convoy. The Germans, who saw a package on the road, approached me.

"Get up!" I heard a shout.

I didn't respond.

"Get up!" someone shouted again.

I didn't respond and I didn't breath.

He hit me with a stick. Despite the intense pain I did not move.

"He's dead." I heard another voice.

"He is alive." the second one said.

"He's dead." the first repeated, and kicked me hard.

They didn't care if I was really alive or dead and they continued on their way.

A while after the sound of footsteps died down, I rolled into a ditch on the side of the road. I again waited several minutes. Silence. I called, not too loudly: "Moshe-Hirsch, Moshe-Hirsch".

Suddenly I saw someone nearby get up and say: "I'm here".

We both lay in the ditch, and curled up in our blankets and waited.

After a while we heard footsteps again. We peeked and saw that a group of prisoners were running on the road. We rose up. When they noticed us, they said that they saw an S.S. *commando* group traveling on the road behind us. "They're killing everybody that they see." they warned.

The only thing we could do to avoid injury, we thought, was to walk in the direction of the transport. If anyone happened upon us we'd say that we were weak and moving slowly in the direction of our transport. The excuse seemed plausible.

We started to move and suddenly we spotted a work-shed, like many spread along the roadside. We approached the building and saw prisoners hiding within who had dropped off or escaped from the transport.

There were 12 men and a dozen opinions about how to act and hide.

Moshe-Hirsch advised that we continue to march in the direction of the transport. Everybody cursed him.

"I was a soldier and I understand a bit about terrain and the army." I told the group.

"I recommend that we break up into small groups, two-three people in each group", I explained. "Each one will go in a different direction." They all agreed.

When everyone spread out, I returned with Moshe-Hirsch to the ditch and we began walking towards the transport. His proposal was the most logical, at least at that time of night. We moved along the road slowly under the cover of darkness.

"Who's there?" we heard a voice that surprised us. We couldn't see who was asking the question.

"We are from the transport that passed through here" we

threw into the void. Gradually we saw two men with weapons opposite us.

"We are sick, so are steps are slow", we explained.

"The transport passed a while ago," they said and pointed in its direction.

We continued and reached a village. There we were also stopped by two armed men. We repeated our mantra and continued onward.

Before we left this village, another two armed men approached us.

"We are from the transport that passed through here." we repeated our story to them as well.

"Shitty transport", they answered and arrested us.

They brought us to the local prison. We told them that we were hungry and they brought us food. At least something had come of this. We met several other prisoners in the jailhouse.

The next morning, they assembled all the prisoners – 12 in number. "We will escort you to the transport." said one of the prison guards who was armed.

We started to walk on the main road. Two guards, who looked quite old and barely carried their weapons, walked slowly. They were apparently from the local civil guard.

On the way we saw a strange sight: civilians with suitcases going from place to place. Chaos was apparent.

I didn't want to continue in this convoy. I decided to escape again. I had no desire to return to the transport.

"I need the bathroom." I told one of the guards.

"Go to the bridge and when you are done join us." he replied and pointed to a bridge.

I nodded my head in agreement and left the convoy.

Moshe-Hirsch immediate understood what I had done. He also needed to relieve himself and within a few minutes joined me. Later I found out that little by little the others abandoned this grotesque convoy. I managed to see the guards returning in the direction of the village empty handed. They didn't appear sorry to lose the guardianship that they had taken upon themselves.

We advanced slowly and reached a nearby village. At the entrance we met a Polish farmer who told us that the Americans would arrive in a day or two. He advised us to hide. We saw woods a short distance away. We decided to move in that direction in order to duck within.

On the way to the woods an S.S. man drove past on a motorcycle. "What are you doing here?" he stopped and asked.

"We are sick and advancing towards the transport slowly." we replied.

"I am going into the city, if I see you again when I return, you know what your fate will be." he said and sped off on his motorcycle.

As soon as he disappeared we started running towards the woods. While looking for a place to hide another farmer, who was plowing his field, saw us. "You'd better get out here and return to the transport immediately." he ordered us. The pistol bulging from his overalls pocket convinced us to obey him.

We began to return to the road. We didn't know which was worse – to meet up again with the threatening motorcyclist or to be wounded by the plowing farmer.

When we were sufficiently far away from the plowing farmer, and we knew that he couldn't see us, we changed direction towards the woods. There were other prisoners already hiding there. We realized that there was no advantage in remaining.

"We should return to the village and look for the farmer who told us that the Americans were on the way." Moshe-Hirsch advised, "Perhaps he will hide us." I agreed with him that this farmer was the only person who hadn't threatened us or chased us away.

We returned to the village that evening. "We are from the transport." we told a group of civilians who gathered at the entrance to the town. We advanced a bit and didn't notice that one of the young girls from the group had disappeared. In retrospect, this reminds me of when I became a POW in 1939 near Bidgoshez. The girl returned with two young Germans, each looking about 25 years old. They both had guns. They stepped alongside us.

"Hands up!" one of them shouted sharply.

We raised our hands.

Both of them searched us for weapons. When they didn't find any, they asked us what we were doing there.

"We are part of the transport that passed through here, we're on its trail." we replied.

"I was a guard at Maidanek", the slightly older one said. It seemed that he was taking command and not really listening to what I said.

What could be better for him – I thought to myself – than to return his lost honor, especially when two victims presented themselves to him.

"According to orders these prisoners are entitled to bread, butter and coffee" he ordered the civilians who looked at us indifferently. Both Moshe-Hirsch and I didn't expect such a reception, especially from a former guard at Maidanek.

The order had to be carried out and food was quickly brought. We were given an opportunity to eat and drink. When we were done, we were led with respect to the local prison. Another 12 prisoners were already there. The room was dark and we felt straw on the floor. The only thing that we knew for certain was the time since there was a grandfather clock in the hall that rang on the hour.

At exactly midnight, as the clock struck twelve, a flashlight flickered by the door. "I am the mayor." said a man who opened the door. We didn't really care who the man was, but he was holding a big pot of food. The pot contained noodles cooked in oil. We ate with our hands. Afterwards he returned and took the pot.

"Don't tell anyone." he said.

Apparently he wanted references of his integrity in preparation for the impending American occupation.

The very same night many of us had an attack of diarrhea. Since we could not exit to the yard, the smelly results were all over our cell. In the morning we were kicked out into the yard, and the Germans brought a water hose and ordered us to wash and dispose of the night's excrement.

Several hours later, we were led in a procession, all 14 of us, in the direction of the transport. Two armed S.S. men accompanied us. One of them walked in front, we followed him and the other S.S. man was at the end of the procession.

While walking I slowed down and approached the guard at the end of the procession. "You can hear the sound of cannons very clearly", I said to him.

"How do you know that it's the sound of cannons?" he asked.

"I was a soldier in the Polish army and I can recognize the sound of cannon fire." I replied.

"It's to your advantage to release us", I told him after another good part of the way. "We will be your recommenders of integrity before the Americans."

The S.S. man thought a moment. Suddenly he ran in the direction of the soldier at the head of the procession. He apparently told him what I had said.

"Come to the head of the line!" the soldier leading the procession commanded me. "If you want to escape, we'll shoot you."

I went to the front of the line and walked behind him. Gradually I slowed down and a gap formed between the procession and the leader. This didn't appear to please the S.S. man. "If you continue to move slowly we won't reach the transport." he said angrily. "It should be clear to all of you what the consequences will be." he added.

Why did he only threaten us? Together with his friend, he could easily have killed us. But that didn't happen.

We continued to progress slowly, and after a few kilometers reached Lezandersleben.

The Germans led us to a huge field filled with hundreds of S.S. soldiers. They left us in the custody of the soldiers and went to the police to report the new "goods" that arrived. After a half hour the soldiers returned and brought us to a prison adjacent to the police station. We were led inside and saw that there were other prisoners. Together we numbered approximately 40 men.

* * *

"What should we do with the prisoners?"

"Shitty prisoners!"

"Shitty, shitty, but what do we do with them?"

"Exactly what we did with those from yesterday!"

"Today too?"

"Yes, today as well!"

Both of them didn't realize that this conversation was being overheard. And perhaps it didn't matter to either of them.

The chaos that took place in the wide parade grounds, situated on the north side of the police station at Lezandersleben, reflected actual situation. Also the muffled sounds of explosions also testified that something was about to happen.

All the way to Lezandersleben, which we passed early that morning, the road was overflowing with convoys of refugees. German civilians who had abandoned their homes were moving eastward. Here and there we saw small groups of German soldiers in uniform, without weapons, walking to the east. Over the last few days this scene had become more commonplace. Like me, they also didn't know what tomorrow would bring. Our hope was great. The reality – not so bright.

No one tried to escape from the procession that led us to Lezandersleben. We innocently believed, or assumed, that this journey would end in freedom. It was obvious to everyone that the war was about to change course. We were moving westward and we had the feeling that we were moving in the direction of freedom. The Germans were retreating and the Americans advancing. It was a matter of hours, we thought.

When we arrived in Lezandersleben we were led respectfully to the police station, and there we were, of course, placed under arrest. A strange routine that we had become accustomed to. The policeman appointed to guard us, an older man in his 50's, immediate provided food and drink. Nice of him, I thought. I'm certain that he was just following orders. This same soldier was not fulfilling his guard duties. Maybe he was tired of all the commotion. For example, we could go to the toilet in the yard without limitations. The condition was that two could not leave together. Until the first returned the next in line could not leave.

Even before we settled in the cell the rotation of those leaving began. Some actually needed to use the latrine, but others wanted to breathe fresh air and see what was happening.

"Curious, eh?" the policeman remarked when he realized that our bladders were over-active. But it didn't appear to bother him as long as the order he had established was kept.

The first time I went to relieve my bladder I managed to see that the police station fence was breached, and if I wanted to escape there wouldn't be a problem. There was a great bustling of soldiers, policemen, and civilians in one place. It appeared to me that there was no lack of chaos. It was obvious that we, the prisoners, who were dressed in our tattered clothes so differently than those surrounding us, didn't influence their activities. The well-known striped pajamas, that were torn and worn out, were still the only garment for most of us. I was still wearing the coat that was stained by the blood of the Ukrainian, killed during of the bombing of the train that carried us from Buchenwald.

The need for order meant that I had to return to the jail cell until the next hoped-for turn. Escape meant hurting a friend. It was on my second trip to the latrine that I witnessed the conversation I had described earlier.

At first I didn't think it related to me and my fate. It was more relevant to the group of prisoners. Also the two speakers, a civilian of about 35 who held a weapon in his left hand, and a German officer younger than him who apparently gave the orders there, ignored me totally, and perhaps actually didn't see me.

I heard the conversation but I hadn't internalized it. Before returning to the cell, I also saw a great commotion beyond the border of the police station yard. Convoys of citizens were traveling in all directions. The echoing noise of bombs that we had heard in the last few days now sounded closer than ever before, as if across the street. At this stage it didn't appear that the sounds of bombing bothered those doing their business in the yard. Nobody looked for cover. In one of the corners I saw a barrel billowing thick smoke, and soldiers stood nearby and dumped piles of documents inside. Soldiers and civilians kept arriving with documents that they piled near the barrel.

Destroying evidence, I thought innocently.

I returned to the cell to let the next man catch a breather and I waited impatiently for my next turn. I hated being locked up. The conversation in the cell encouraged hope, the end of the war might actually be coming. Everyone felt that they would soon be released and couldn't wait to be free.

But no one could imagine how this event would actually play out. Just before my turn came again, the door to the jail cell opened wide and two German soldiers standing at the threshold ordered us to leave quickly and climb up onto a truck, whose rear door was flush against the entrance to the police station. It seemed to me that they didn't wait for one of the prisoners who took his turn in the latrine. The policeman who was guarding us was also surprised by their sudden appearance, and did not alert them that one prisoner was delayed in returning. It didn't seem to bother anyone.

In passing from the dark jail cell to the truck the bright light blinded us, and we couldn't see the contents of the truck.

"Where are they taking us?" we heard someone ask the policeman who escorted us until the entrance to the truck.

"I don't know." replied the policeman in a kind of apology. He had already managed to establish friendships with the prisoners he was guarding.

"Where are they taking us?" the same voice insisted and this time addressed one of the soldiers.

"Silence!" we heard him scream. "Not a word! Speaking is forbidden!"

"Shit." one of the prisoners whispered, but his voice echoed inside the space.

As soon as I climbed up, the last prisoner in line, a canvas covering was lowered. Total darkness prevailed inside. Here and there were cracks where light rays poked through, but it wasn't enough to illuminate the truck's cargo area. We heard the cabin doors slam shut and the truck began to move.

After a few minutes of travel I felt a strange bustle inside the truck. Someone situated inside the truck noticed that it was also carrying three soldiers and a machine gun. The same person alerted his traveling neighbor, and very quickly it became obvious to all of us that this was our last journey.

"They're taking us out to be killed." a prisoner said with a trembling voice.

"Silence here!" was shouted in German.

Nobody opened their mouth. Once again the butcher's knife circled above my head.

The muffled sound of explosions heard in the jail cell and the station yard became stronger and louder.

I pushed up against a crack in the canvas covering and tried to determine which way we were going. It seemed to me that the truck was turning to the west, and went off the main road to one of the paths. A small but dense wood appeared some distance away. The truck approached these woods. Near the woods I saw a threshing granary that the truck was forced to pass slowly. The truck entered a curve and slowed down, perhaps to stop.

Suddenly an intense bomb blast shocked the truck's cargo space. We felt as if we had been blown off the carriage. The truck continued to move a few meters, tipped slightly on its side, and stopped. A warm wave began to spread within the space. The canvas cover was immediately removed. I remember that within seconds I jumped outside and found myself with several more prisoners in a ditch close by the granary and the burning truck. Two soldiers who jumped after us from inside the truck started moving eastward using the path we had traveled on several minutes beforehand. I assumed that a shell had fallen between the truck and the granary and its ricochet set fire to the granary and also destroyed the front of the truck.

"If they are moving eastward, we shall move westward!" I said to Moshe-Hirsch who was beside me, and I pointed in the direction opposite to that of the two distancing Germans. We quickly jumped to another ditch nearby the path, and we hid. The rest of the people remained in the first ditch.

* * *

A silence prevailed after the Germans fled. A silence in sharp contrast to what had taken place a few minutes earlier. Perhaps someone had tried to target the truck, and when they succeeded – went quiet.

Only some hours later did the muffled sounds of explosions again dominate the atmosphere for a short interval. From a distance we could see the light traffic of vehicles we couldn't identify and people carrying portable items who marched eastward.

A solitary tank could also be seen west of where we stood. Maybe this was who had shelled the truck?

We waited until dark. Before sunset, with the last crimson light, we entered the woods. There were dozens of recently dead bodies strewn among the trees, prisoners still in their pajamas who had been shot at close range.

"They tried to escape." Moshe-Hirsch said to me as we entered deep into the woods. It was clear to both of us that we were almost destined to be exactly there, and in the same state, a few hours beforehand.

* * *

We were liberated the following morning.

Later I learned that all the prisoners who were in the jail house with us were released by the Americans, except for the one prisoner caught in the latrine rotation at the police station. He was shot at Lezandersleben.

The Final Night?

With nightfall Moshe-Hirsch and I entered the thicket of woods. We were certain that this was the best place to spend the night. The surrounding silence hid what was about to happen.

The bodies we encountered were only located on the edge of the woods. Deep inside we neither heard nor saw anything. We found a comfortable hiding place and lay down on the ground. I tried to fall asleep but couldn't. Moshe-Hirsch couldn't fall asleep either. It was cold and we were hungry and thirsty.

"I am going over to the truck." I told Moshe-Hirsch, "I may find something there to eat".

"Are you crazy?" he said.

"I'm so thirsty that I need to look for something", I answered.

"I'm staying here." he said.

I marked his location and moved slowly towards the truck. Alongside the truck, clearly visible as a foreign object in the surroundings, I saw the driver's body. It was sprawled, and from the way it laid no one appeared to have touched it. He was apparently killed instantly. The door of the truck was broken open, and it was obvious that someone had already visited there. The cabin was messed up by those who had groped around.

Someone beat me to it, I thought. Nonetheless I climbed up onto the truck and stretched my hand towards the glove compartment. It was locked or damaged from the heat of the shell-strike. I tried to force it open and didn't succeed. I looked for something to use to break it open and found a metal bar. I didn't want to raise a commotion. Who knows who was still in the area. With the aid of the bar I bent the cover of the compartment and slowly broke it open. I was sure that I'd find something there, and so I wasn't surprised when I found a salami sandwich and a thermos. I took the treasure, as well as two torn blankets, and followed my tracks back into the woods.

"Pssst Pssst", I heard Moshe-Hirsch directing me towards him. "When you left here someone passed through." he said. "I wasn't sure if he saw you or me so I changed the location."

I showed him the treasure. We divided the food and drink. Everything vanished within minutes. We dumped the thermos. Out of fear. Yes, fear that we may have been caught with something German in our possession. Who knew what would happen tomorrow?

After the rich meal we had lain upon the ground and fell into a deep sleep.

* * *

"Where are you from?" I heard a German voice demanding while a powerful flashlight beamed in my face. I covered my eyes with my hand and couldn't see who was asking.

"Where is there an airport?" the voice continued in a very angry tone.

I suspected that I was about to become a guide, and for a German of all people...

"Why are you looking for an airport?" I managed to ask before the light was diverted from my eyes. Through the blur of my eyelids and the fingers of my hand I saw a German officer wearing what seemed to me like an air force uniform.

"Where is there an airport?" the German repeated his

question, and this time it sounded somewhat different, with exasperation filtering through.

"The Americans are here!" I said with some anger, and I thought that would impress him.

"Shitty Americans!" he said, and continued on his way.

I stared at his receding shadow and managed to see that he had no weapon.

"What luck." Moshe-Hirsch said with a sigh, as he awoke upon hearing the conversation.

The darkness was almost total and it wasn't cold under the blankets.

It was the night of April 13, 1945. The place, near Lezander-sleben.

Before we managed to dispense with this intrusion, "the German Pilot", as Moshe-Hirsch and I nicknamed him after-wards, we heard footsteps that were definitely approaching us.

"Give me your food", we heard a Russian voice insist with a heavy Ukrainian accent. I hated them. They were the worst during the *actzias* and in the camps. "People eaters", we called them. They behaved most violently towards us, and many of them succeeded where the Germans had not.

"Just what I need, I thought. A Ukrainian, and hungry as well!

"We have no food." I heard Moshe-Hirsch answer him.

"We have to get away from him." I whispered to Moshe-Hirsch in Yiddish.

He heard that I spoke but did not understand.

"Bring me food." he shouted and closed in on us.

"We don't have food." Moshe-Hirsch repeated his answer.

"Pull down the blankets." he ordered.

We each removed our blankets. As he stared a while, he apparently realized that his salvation would not come from us. We looked so pathetic, covered with torn blankets, dressed in worn out clothing, and we were surely not the address he was looking for.

"What a disaster." he spat out in Russian and continued on his way.

I couldn't manage to fall asleep again despite my desperate attempts.

* * *

When dawn rose we wrapped ourselves in blankets and prepared to make our steps in the direction of the nearby town.

"You, Jews." we suddenly heard a voice, before even leaving the woods. We turned around. To our dismay we saw a group of German soldiers in uniform standing behind us.

"Just what we really need now." I heard Moshe-Hirsch whisper my thoughts.

"We know that you are Jews." said the apparent leader of the group. None of them possessed weapons. They were probably going to voluntary captivity.

"We are going there." I pointed towards the city. "When we see the Americans we'll tell them that you are here." I'm not sure that they understood what I had said. It seemed that most of them were bothered by something else.

Right after I said that sentence I felt relieved. For the first time in many years I didn't fear the Germans. Here I was standing before them as equals. A few hours earlier I had felt their threat. And quite suddenly, with the dawn, the threat passed as if it had never existed.

The Germans continued westward, and we, Moshe-Hirsch and I, left the woods alongside the burnt-out truck.

In the outskirts of town we noticed an isolated house. "Let's enter the house", I said to Moshe, "Maybe we'll manage to shower and shave." The sensation that morning was totally different. Were we going to be liberated? If so, then it paid to be clean and presentable.

I knocked on the door. "Can we have something to drink?" I inquired in German.

"The Germans are returning." a woman answered from behind the locked door.

Neither of us had the strength to argue with her.

The prevailing quiet since the previous nightfall hinted to us that the town had probably fallen into American hands.

"What will happen if the Germans shoot at us?" asked Moshe-Hirsch.

"Let's take off our undershirts and hang them on something." I said.

We found two branches of sufficient length and hung the remains of our undershirts upon them. They were filthy. The white color had disappeared long ago, but our intention was clear.

At the town's entrance we saw two armed civilians. They stared at us and called us over.

"Did we make a mistake?" I asked Moshe-Hirsch. "Do we have to claim again that we are following the transport?"

He didn't manage to reply. It seemed that the two were surprised to see us so early and waving white flags at that.

"The Americans are in town." one of them said in German, with a French accent, and pointed towards the city center. "They will already receive you in an orderly manner."

On the way into the town we saw several American tanks for the first time and it was relatively smaller than what I knew. American soldiers stood next to the tank and stared at the ghostly spirits who were carrying flags made from rags that were hung upon branches. They didn't seem to care about us. They stared at us and continued to deal with something else.

We didn't know English. We approached them and stood. We tried to attract their attention. I recall that we lowered our "flags" and stood alongside them. This time they got closer to us. I didn't know what to do. I felt a great embarrassment. What do you do? How do you describe who we are? How do you summarize with a word, a gesture, what we had endured these last few years?

I made up my mind. I stretched out my arm and revealed my number to them. I thought that this would say something to them. I was certain that they knew why they were on German soil. With one gesture I tried to summarize everything.

They stared at me, at my arm, at the number, and did not understand what I had meant.

"Jew." I said in German. Maybe this would shake them out of their indifference. It didn't seem to impress them.

"Jew." I said in Yiddish. This also didn't help.

"Jew." I said in Polish and afterwards in Russian.

It didn't appear to me that they took the hint.

Suddenly a soldier leaped from behind them bringing several slices of bread that he gave to us. I looked at Moshe-Hirsch, and he at me, and we decided to take the bread. Happily, we weren't so hungry and we held the bread in our hands.

The Americans gestured that we continue in the direction of the town center but without the flag. We thanked them in Yiddish and walked in that direction.

We entered the town. It appeared abandoned. We were the only ones walking in the street. While walking along I saw an abandoned Volkswagen vehicle, its doors wide open and on the front seat there was a bottle of cognac and a loaf of bread that appeared fresh, compared to what I had known in the camps.

What an effort it had taken me only a short while ago to get a bottle of cognac or a loaf of bread, I thought to myself, and here, quite suddenly, just such a treasure fell upon me. I was afraid to touch the treasure. I thought that if I touched it they may have shot at me. Perhaps someone was looking at us and waiting. Someone wanted us to fail.

Moshe-Hirsch also saw the treasure. I looked around us and didn't see a living soul. We decided, although with some hesitation, to take the food. We were not hungry, but we hadn't drunk cognac in quite a while.

I opened the bottle and gulped the intoxicating drink. "Where am I? Where am I?" I immediately asked Moshe-Hirsch. I felt a kind of warm explosion rising from my throat and to my head and an immense confusion. Did I actually get drunk? I felt that my feet could not carry me.

Luckily for me, Moshe-Hirsch didn't manage to drink. He helped me to sit down and forced me to eat bread. I don't know if it was a slice from the American bread or a cut from the loaf that was in the car.

"We can go on." I said after a few minutes. "I feel alright." We approached the center of town.

* * *

I felt true liberation with the changing of clothes. In the center of town, nearby an American equipment truck, I shed the prisoner's clothing that I had received several weeks earlier and the coat which was stained with the Ukrainian's blood, and I dressed in civilian's clothing that I received from the Americans.

Moshe Brezniak, born in Mezritch, a soldier in the Polish Army, prisoner number 127942, was being released.

First Period of Liberation

How can one describe the soul's elation during the passage from darkness to light, from horror and hell to hope, from being caged to liberty, or simply from imprisonment to freedom? Is revenge the first emotion that arises within you? Why not? Why not go and seek revenge? If so – from who? How? Alone or together with someone?

* * *

The first thing I wanted to do when I was liberated was to thank the person who had given me my last meal in captivity. It was the mayor of the neighboring town, or so he claimed, who had brought cooked food for us in the jail cell late at night. Most of us had gotten diarrhea from this cooked food, but.... to receive food from a German, and by his initiative? During the entire last period I hadn't encountered any human consideration like that. Until then when I received food it was due to an order. But to receive food from someone's independent initiative, and a German after all? The only initiative that they had demonstrated was in the field of vicious destruction, competing with each other to see who was more original in transferring us to the next world.

Both of us, Moshe-Hirsch and I, strode toward the town. Traffic between Lezandersleben and this town was very light. Here and there we saw a farmer traveling, maybe to a field, or a vehicle with American soldiers. No one stopped us along the way.

When we arrived in town and asked to see the mayor, we realized that we were late. He had apparently feared the Americans and fled to the East. We couldn't thank him, and didn't have the opportunity to commend his last moment of righteousness.

We returned to Lezandersleben. The number of prisoners moving in the direction of the American center increased. We, who already dressed in civilian clothes, could direct them in the appropriate direction.

Suddenly I realized that there were trees in town with birds upon them, and there were stores (closed however), and there were colors, and we could circulate without fear. A special feeling of freedom.

The Germans who remained in the town offered us lodging in their houses. The fear of spending the night with a German family had disappeared. I spent the night with the brother of the mayor of Lezandersleben, and Moshe-Hirsch found a place with the nearby neighbor, whose husband was still in the army and hadn't returned yet.

* * *

On the first of May, about two weeks after liberation, we were still in Lezandersleben. The feeling of freedom had already assumed new dimensions. The Russians soldiers who congregated there, local civilians, and liberated soldiers celebrated the holiday – the workers holiday. In the years preceding the war, a parade or big demonstration was always the central focus of the holiday. Although there was no parade this time the Russians, who had organized the event, ushered those invited into the municipality hall for a party. We, members of the Jewish group, were also invited to celebrate. I recall at the party they sang ballads honoring Lenin and Stalin, and many of the Russians drank to intoxication.

During the event a Russian officer approached me and asked me to leave the hall. I didn't know why he had turned to me.

"Do you see them?" he said, "All those who sing for Stalin and Lenin," he remained quiet a moment and afterwards continued, "When they were in captivity, they were the first to expose the Jews and as a result your Jewish brothers were sent by the Germans to their death." he concluded.

"Why are you telling me this?", I questioned.

"I am a Jew and I know that you are a Jew", adding, "And they", he pointed inside, "they don't know."

"Come with us, escape from them." I offered.

Our group increased and grew every day.

"I'll think about it." he replied.

Later on, when the opportunity arose, he hopped onto a train for Russia.

* * *

I cannot say that the desire for revenge had disappeared completely. We tried. How?

In Lezandersleben we met a German citizen who had been a political prisoner in Buchenwald because he was a declared communist. This same German told us that the mayor of the nearby town actively sent all those who had opposed the regime to work camps. He requested that we try to make sure that he didn't retain his position under the new American military government. "He must be punished." he said.

Since he was afraid to carry out the mission himself he involved us. We decided to include him in our group and seek revenge.

The following morning we approached one of the local

farmers to borrow his wagon and horse and then headed towards the nearest big city, to the regional American military headquarters. When we arrived, we requested to meet the local commander. His secretary barred us from meeting him.

"Why is it so important to meet him?" asked the clerk, who was the first female soldier we had seen saw in an American uniform.

"We have information about the mayor of the neighboring town who is responsible for the 'transfer' of many civilians to Buchenwald for political reasons." we explained. "The man still serves as the town mayor and he must be punished."

The secretary listened to us and then entered the commander's office. We waited outside.

"You don't need to get involved in politics." she said, turned and left.

And thus my active stage of revenge was finished. Occasional thoughts of vengeance occurred to me, but action did not.

* * *

The public responsibility of the brother of Lezandersleben's mayor, who was housing me, involved electricity, water and sewage in the city and its surroundings.

"The main engine of the pump that supplies the city's water was damaged during the bombing." he told me one morning, knowing that I was an electrician. "Would you be willing to try to repair it?" he asked.

Should I help them? This dilemma crossed my mind. They should be buried, from my point of view – they should die of thirst. Again the feeling of revenge arose. But it immediately faded. Indeed I am not a vengeful man. I went to the pumphouse with him and after hard day of work, I managed to get the pump working again to supply water for the inhabitants of this German city.

* * *

The feeling of liberation and freedom were truly special. The general atmosphere in the city was of elation. Food was not lacking, and we were, of course, not required to work. The municipality and its chief took care of all our needs.

In the month following our release about 40 Jews reached the city. It was easy to identify us. We were very comfortable together. Just yesterday we had been the target of annihilation. Not any more today. We organized ourselves into a typical group. Since I was one of the first in town, and was close to the mayor, I was nominated to be the group spokesman. The city hall had divided the liberated prisoners into groups in order to distribute food. This made it easier for the municipality workers. Instead of working opposite many people, they could work opposite group leaders.

At first they attempted to attach us to a Polish group, and to feed us together with them. "We've had enough of Poles", I told the mayor. He nodded his head with understanding and decided that we would be a separate group.

* * *

On May 2nd the news spread that we could return home.

Home? What was home for me? I thought. My whole family was gone. My father had been killed in either Trevniki or Maidanek, my brother Zeev had been killed on the train, Naphtali and his family had been killed in either Lublin or Maidanek, all my uncles and aunts had died, some in Treblinka and others in Maidanek. The strongest among them had reached Auschwitz and perished, either there or in Birkenau. Chaim was in Australia and Uncle Anatol Gelberg was in the United States.

I had no home in Europe ! I couldn't bear to think about it.

"My home is in Eretz Yisrael ", I told my group of colleagues. "I'll never return to Poland and my house in Mezritch!"

"You do not have Israeli citizenship", was the bureaucratic reply, "each of you must return to your house, where you come from!", thus they shut up all the spokesmen.

"Only there, to Eretz Yisrael, we will go", I and several others in the group insisted.

"We will inquire", the municipality officials replied.

The next day we received permission from the authorities of the liberating army to begin our journey to Eretz Yisrael. And because they cared? They wanted to be rid of the burden of being liberators and to return quickly to a normal life. The war was over, now they began to live again, and it was preferable without strangers.

The Journey to Eretz Yisrael

"You are going to France," said the American officer who was responsible for transportation. "Look for the train that is traveling to France," he added, "They'll take care of you there."

"To France?" I questioned.

"You will reach Eretz Yisrael from there," the officer said, "Boats sail for Eretz Yisrael from Marseille, on the Mediterranean coast."

Not all 40 members of the group wanted to immigrate to Eretz Yisrael. Some returned to Poland, others decided to remain in Germany, but the majority decided to go southward to France.

On May 13th 1945 the mayor arranged a truck to take us to the train station. There we mounted, without paying of course, the train for France. I remember seeing the name "Paris" written on the car. Travel on the entire train system was free at that time.

My memory of the last train I had traveled on, the one bombed by the British, was still fresh. How much time had passed? I thought to myself. This time conditions on the train were completely different from those trips to the camps. We were traveling as humans on a passenger train again. And there was food for everybody on the train. Nothing was missing.

During the trip I gazed at the German pastoral countyside and thought about the ups and downs of life.

The next day, when we arrived at Liege in Belgium we were

ordered to disembark from the train that continued to Paris. I organized a rebellion.

"We aren't leaving the train in Belgium," I said to the Belgian who wore an unrecognizable uniform.

"You must disembark," he said politely.

"We are traveling to Eretz Yisrael," I insisted.

"Only French citizens are permitted to travel on the train to Paris", he explained. "Whoever isn't a French citizen will be forcefully removed at the border". That is what he said. I wasn't certain that he understood the words 'Eretz Yisrael'.

"Let them force us off!" I challenged.

The group members vocally agreed with my struggle. "Don't agree to leave." they said to each other in Yiddish.

"I will make sure that you are forcibly removed." the man said, still pleasantly.

"Let them try."

"I'll summon the local police." he warned impatiently. "Listen, the situation in France is terrible. There is serious famine everywhere, and the French government has decided to care for its own citizens first." he breathed heavily. "You do not have French citizenship and therefore you cannot enter France. They shall pull you off at the border and not take care of you. Here at least someone can care for all your needs as refugees." he clarified his position.

I understood that perhaps there was no choice and we had to obey him. I translated his words from German to Yiddish. The revolt disintegrated and we willingly stepped down from the train.

We left the station and walked to the camp set up in the city center. There were not only Jews in the group. There were also other refugees without Belgian citizenship, as well as Belgian citizens who were allowed to return to their homes. We remained in the camp.

I didn't like the idea of returning to a camp, although this was an open camp and our treatment was good. Food and housing was, of course, free of charge. We also received pocket money in the local currency. We could circulate freely within the camp or beyond its borders, whereas we would spend the night there. Not everyone. There was no head count. Whoever found lodging outside the camp could stay in town.

* * *

In Liege I heard that there was a field in central Brussels where refugees and survivors assembled to search for their loved ones. I thought to myself, that perhaps I'd have a chance to find someone from my extended family, or at least hear about someone who was still alive. Maybe there was still a possibility after all. Following several days of feeling uneasy and indecisive I made up my mind to reach Brussels on my own.

There was a strong attraction to this field for me. I had already gotten what I could out of the camp at Liege. I thought that in Brussels the future would be rosier. The dream to reach Eretz Yisrael did not fade but in fact intensified, and I thought that Brussels was a better place to try to realize it. So one day I caught a train for Brussels.

As soon as I arrived in the big city I proceeded to look for the field. It wasn't difficult to find. My optimistic mood disappeared instantly. The scene was among the saddest that I had ever seen. Boys, girls, men and women were clutching photographs of their loved ones whom they were searching for, and asking everyone they encountered if they had seen or heard anything regarding the people in each picture. Great sadness was visible in their eyes. Desperation permeated the air.

When you are deep inside the horror it is hard to comprehend just how bad the situation is. Now, after the war, I began to understand the magnitude of the terrible destruction that the Germans had wrought. Hundreds and thousands passed through that field, and they were all looking for something to grasp on to. It was an awful sight.

In the wide field one could identify different political groups among the Jews. There were communists, *Hashomer Hatzair* people, Beitarists (Revisionists) and so on. There was also a kitchen to feed the needy. And who wasn't needy?

That evening I returned to Liege by train. The bundle of emotions possessing me had completely changed.

"I am not remaining here." I told the group members.

"Where are you going?" I was asked.

"To Brussels." I replied.

"What's there?"

"A future and life." I answered. "Whoever wants to come with me is invited." I added. As if I could host someone.

At night I described to the group what I had seen in Brussels. It was not difficult to convince them to join me. The next morning we were on the train to Brussels. Menachem Averbach, a friend from the camps, was also in the group.

When we arrived in Brussels, I directed my friends to the field. I already felt at home. I strolled in the field and searched for acquaintances, but didn't find anyone.

In one of the corners of the field I saw someone carrying the *Hashomer Hatzair* flag. Something awoke within me upon seeing it. I still felt allegiance to the movement that had nurtured my love for Eretz Yisrael. I approached him and we began a conversation.

"I arrived in Brussels from Poland a few months before the war broke out and I married a local girl." he explained. "The war forced me to separate from my wife who moved to one of the Belgian villages, to a local family, and I joined a non-Jewish family in the city, received a different identity, and thus survived the war. My wife still hasn't returned, and I have a big apartment." he added, inviting Menachem and myself to live with him.

I remained in Brussels for several weeks. My stay provided an excellent recovery after an incurable disease – the war.

We were a young group, without any obligations, in a foreign city. We were not required to work, food and housing was provided without cost, and we also received pocket money. We enjoyed seeing many places. Sex was plentiful. Women and men mutually felt that they had lost a period in their lives and they wanted to compensate themselves for lost time.

Despite the good life the dream of traveling to Eretz Yisrael did not fade. I exerted enormous pressure on acquaintances with local influence, to get us permission to immigrate legally, with certificates. We heard of the illegal immigration but we knew that it was also possible to immigrate legally. After many efforts, we eventually managed to make the proper connections that secured our certificates.

The tasks of the Jewish Agency in Brussels, and those of *Hashomer Hatzair* that operated through it, was varied; these included helping Jews immigrate to Eretz Yisrael.

The British authorities agreed to unify families. Family unification enabled parents of children who lived in Palestine, or children from parents who lived in Palestine, to submit requests to the British authorities. If approved, they could receive certificates. We called this legal immigration. Before the war we were already aware of the existence of illegal immigration.

Not being the son of or the father of anyone, I had no chance for legal immigration to Eretz Yisrael. Nonetheless I insisted. I appealed to the *Hashomer Hatzair* organization in Brussels, presented myself, explained to them that I was in Zionist training before the war, and expressed my intense desire to immigrate to Eretz Yisrael.

One day I was called to the *Hashomer Hatzair* center and told that they had acquired a certificate for me. I had to show up on a particular day at the train station in town, to leave for Paris. To my relief, Menachem Averbach had also received a certificate.

* * *

During my stay in Brussels I wrote a letter to my brother Chaim who lived in Australia and my uncle Anatol Gelberg who lived in the United States. The letters were written in French because the local censors forbad the sending of letters in German or Yiddish. After a several weeks I received replies from each of them. Chaim invited me to Australia and Uncle Anatol wanted me to come to the United States. I answered both that it was my desire to live among Jews. Their letters arrived a day or two after I knew that my path to Eretz Yisrael was paved, and I felt a certain confidence. But for that I would have probably traveled to the other end the earth.

* * *

I recall Paris as a burden. We stayed four days as guests of the Agency in one of the hotels that they had rented for this purpose. From Paris we went by train to Toulouse, where there was a military port used by British war vessels. The immigrants to Eretz Yisrael were housed in vacant spots on the warship "Mata Hari", that was in the Royal Navy service. Jewish Agency activity was visible everywhere. Even on the ship, where the number of certificate recipients was limited, the Agency managed to sneak illegal immigrants onboard.

During the voyage the British sailors ignored our presence. Each day drills were conducted that imitated battle conditions, including alarms, shooting and so on. We were prohibited from walking around most areas of the ship.

After a few days of sailing, we arrived in Haifa. It seemed to me that this was the first ship that had arrived after the war bringing legal immigrants to Eretz Yisrael. Before us many illegal survivors had landed, but there was no legal immigration under the British flag.

The ship that brought me to Israel also carried Menachem Averbach and Mr. Schiffer, who I met in Brussels.

* * *

His son Shuki studied together with you in the New High School 21 years later.

First Days in Eretz Yisrael

Many reporters waited at the port to meet survivors coming "from there". This was the first time I had heard the phrase "from there". It seemed to me that the reporters were not interested in a description of our experiences. They didn't want to interview us or hear details of our war. They were more interested in the fate of the Jewish people. They wanted to know more general things and less personal stories. A survivor who wished to tell, to pour out his heart and share his bitter fate with another person, encountered a hostile wall of refusal to listen. Since the situation in Eretz Yisrael during the war was not great, when survivors began to describe their suffering the reaction was often: "Do you know what I went through?"

From Haifa we were transported to Atlit. During the two days that I stayed in the transit camp in Atlit I met local *Hashomer Hatzair* activists. They interviewed me and referred me to Kibbutz Ein Hamifratz, north of Haifa.

Before my trip to the kibbutz I decided to see Haifa. On the bus to Haifa the traveler next to me asked me where I had come from. When I replied that I was from Poland, from Mezritch, he told me that there was a restaurant in the city owned by people who had also come from Mezritch. When he recalled their name I knew that he was speaking about my brother Chaim's friend.

When I arrived in Haifa I left the bus and made my way to

the restaurant. I presented myself and the restaurant owner got very excited. I remember that I told him about his two sisters – Gila and Rita – whom I had seen in Maidanek. He received me graciously and told me that the Wiener family was located in Haifa, and they had apparently changed their name to Tirosh. I knew the Wiener family from Mezritch very well. The restaurant owner took me to them.

They couldn't contain their excitement. I stayed with them about ten days. In fact I had been in Maidanek with Shula Wiener and we were very close. I recall that the family's mother, before immigrating to Israel, was very beautiful, and had even earned the title "Miss Zakopane".

After I left the Wiener family I returned to Atlit. There I met the sister of Moshe-Hirsch Eidelboim, with whom I had endured the end of the war. I had a letter for her in my knapsack which I delivered to her. Moshe-Hirsch remained in Belgium since he couldn't receive a certificate and immigrated to Israel later on. Moshe-Hirsch's sister told me that relatives of the Reinwein family, Yenta and Yosef, were in Ramat Gan.

* * *

The next day I traveled to Ein Hamifratz with the goal of starting a new life in Eretz Yisrael. I thought that what had been interrupted before the war in Poland, regarding training, could restart anew in Israel. I thought that a real-world environment would yield a different meaning and provide substance to my life once again.

The shock of joining the communal life darkened my mood. Suddenly I found myself living together with other people. Of course, the surroundings, the goal, and the freedom were new concepts. But I, who had lived approximately five years with many partners, without my own corner, without being physically alone in almost any situation, where everything was done in the company of others, in a crowd, under pressure, in poverty, wretched, with fear, suddenly found myself living communally again. I wanted a little quiet, not to hear the other speaking, his snoring. I wanted to feel free with myself and to myself. Life in the kibbutz did not allow that.

What really drove me crazy was the morning wake-up call. I am not certain, but suddenly these voices or the noise of the wake-up call seemed to convince me that I was in a concentration camp again. I couldn't rid myself of this irritated feeling.

These memories and thoughts tipped the scales and I decided to leave the kibbutz. I believe that I stayed in Ein Hamifratz only ten days. I requested a short vacation in Tel Aviv and received permission from the kibbutz secretariat.

* * *

The following day I traveled to Moshe-Hirsch Eidelboim's sister who lived in Tel Aviv. She was my only address in Tel Aviv. She also knew my relatives in the city. In fact, she took me to the Reinwein family in Ramat Gan.

We arrived at their house in the evening. Only their son Eliav, Ohad Naharin's father, was at home. The other sons, Avraham and Naphtali, were still in the British Army. Yosef and Yenta were absent because at that moment they were attending a meeting held by the committee of Israeli immigrants from Mezritch. Eliav took me under his wing, and released Moshe-Hirsch's sister. He accompanied me on a trip to Tel Aviv to meet Yenta and Yosef.

The center for immigrants from Mezritch in Israel was in a rooftop apartment located on the Tel Aviv-Yaffo Road. Malcha Barak and her husband, who both came from our city, lived in that rooftop flat, above their work. The apartment's porch served as a meeting place for "Mezritch'aim" and active members of the organization.

238

Yosef and Yenta were overjoyed by my arrival. I waited there until the end of the meeting. Actually, the whole sequence of events until that moment seemed strange to me. I liked the tempo, the meetings with people I knew, family, and other unexpected events. For the first time I began to like the new life in Eretz Yisrael. The freedom and 'rising up' (Aliyah, Hebrew for immigration) acquired true meaning.

While sitting on that roof in Tel Aviv, in August 1945, I decided in my heart to remain in the city, in the center of the country.

When the meeting was over, I went with Yenta and Yosef back to their house. Zehava Berger, the cousin of both Yosef and my mother, was already waiting for me at the Reinwein's home. Someone had passed by her house and informed her of my arrival.

I spent that night with the Reinweins. The next day I went to the kibbutz with Barish Berger, Zehava's husband, and Eliezer Farbman. Barish remained in Haifa and Eliezer helped me to retrieve my bundle of possessions from the kibbutz.

At the end of August 1945, after being a kibbutznik for several days, I became a kibbutz abandoner. Two titles that I never used again.

I returned to the Reinwein family. Although I was received very warmly I decided to look for living quarters that I could rent. Zehava and Barish offered me a room in their apartment on Levontin Street in Tel Aviv, in exchange for rent. The day after receiving the offer I moved in with them.

For the first time in a very long while, I had my own room. Although the kitchen and bathroom were communal, I had a place where I could be by myself.

* * *

The first practical step towards assimilating in the new society was to register with the local employment bureau. To the question "What is your profession?", I answered that I was a certified electrician.

"And what is your level?" I was asked.

"High." I said.

"Diplomas please."

"I have none."

"We must check your professional level." I was told.

"Fine." I replied.

"You must be examined in a practical test to determine your qualifications," they clarified the significance of the test. "You must appear on thus-and-thus date in so-and-so's store and they shall examine you."

I immediately agreed and received the appropriate documents.

"This is not how you come to an exam." said the store owner when I presented the official document.

"Why?"

"Where are your work clothes?" he questioned. "Where are your tools? How do you dare to come to a test this way?" He appeared to really be insulted by me. How and where from should I have work clothes? And even more so, tools?

"Please, examine me and give me the degree that you want." I begged the store owner and his assistant who came to see who had angered the boss. "Try me for one day and prove what I know." I said confidently. It appeared that he understood, from my body language, that I am a positive person, and agreed to test me.

The assistant helped me to fill in some forms, and afterwards began a personal interview in which he asked what I did after completing my studies and during the war. I described in detail all my professional experiences. I tried not to exaggerate. To tell the truth, during the period in which I lived with the Reinwein family and walked around and looked at the electrician's work being done at building sites, I saw that I could perform their jobs, and perhaps even better. At first I thought that in the five years of war there were big developments in that area, but I established that this wasn't the case.

After the interviewer heard of the kinds of systems that I had maintained at Buna and other locations, he skipped the practical exam and gave me level 'A-A'.

"Perhaps you'd like to work with us in the store?" he asked at the end of the interview, after he gave me my degree.

"I am not certain and I still don't know what I want to do." I replied, "Meanwhile I don't want to decide". I didn't want to bind myself to work I wasn't familiar with on the very first day.

I returned to the employment bureau with an 'A-A' electrician's diploma. From the bureau clerk I requested that if he receives a call for new employees from the Electric Company, that he should reach me even if I had started working at another job.

The next day the bureau referred me to two brothers for work, an engineer and an electrical contractor, who had won a contract in the Kfar Azar region. They were constructing a housing complex for Jewish soldiers who were released from the British Army. After a few days I received a notice inviting me for a trial period at the Electric Company. I informed the engineers that I was leaving. They attempted to convince me to stay and even raised my salary above that of a foreman – 125 'grushim' (cents in Mandate currency) a day instead of the 90 'grushim' that I had received until then. None the less I was not convinced. The salary in the Electric Company was 75 'grushim' per day, much lower, but this was work in a large company and not with a small business owner. Even in Mezritch I had worked in the local electric company and liked it. I thought that I could advance in the Electric Company.

When they realized that I was determined to leave the two engineers blessed me and wished me luck.

* * *

In December of 1945 I began working for the Electric Company. They placed me in a group. I felt that the other group members, and the foreman, looked at me like I was an alien. The way I held a hammer, or the way that I bent the metal conduits, was different from what they were accustomed to. After about a week other foreman began visiting to see how I worked. After six months passed I became a permanent employee and was assigned to be a foreman.

In August 1946 I met Tova (Gutta) and in September of that year we married. Until the wedding I lived with Zehava and Barish Berger, and afterwards we rented a dilapidated bungalow in Kiryat Yosef, part of Givataim. When Avi was born in 1948 we rented a room with Natan and Dina Greenberg. After a year we moved with them to an apartment on Hamalben Street in the city. As the family expanded, with the birth of Naphtali and afterwards Sarit, we moved to bigger apartment in the same building. In 1960 we advanced to the apartment in Tel Aviv that we live in today.

Go in Peace, Grandpa Moshe

Prisoner number 127942 Moshe Brezniak has now gone to the next world. Erect. Birch Trees – Brezniak in Polish – upright in their lives and in their death. Whoever was in Auschwitz knows.

"My grandpa was the best ever, that's why he will go to heaven", his 8 year old grand-daughter Adaya wrote in her new ruled notebook this morning. "I know he will go to heaven, I'm certain he will go".

And I, less faithful than she, see him in some kind of metaphoric heaven after all, gently striding among the Birch trees of course, towards the central electric-switch closet – the one without which, we know, the sun does not shine – with pliers and insulation tape in hand, to repair a short-circuit that only he is capable of fixing – and 'hup', let there be light!

Ten year old Roi, who is like his grandfather, busy since birth searching for the "great invention", that when only discovered will cure everything, sees in this death, for the first time, our failure as adults. Here are two doctor sons - Professor Avi and Doctor Naphtali, who know all the secrets of science, a daughter who is an organization advisor – Sarit, who knows how to make order out of every chaos, and their mates: Ori, a computer expert, who knows the most complicated ciphers, Judy a business woman, who offers the best deals, and Micha, a senior journalist with connections and influence in all the right places

– all of them together are not able to overcome the rampage of a single cell in the human system...

So what do I say to him? And to Inbal and Nir, and to Tamar and Sivan, and to Ran and to Ido, and of course to Gutta, who speaks every day with God, and He doesn't really know how to confront the nature gone wild that he himself created.

I'll tell them that we truly tried, and continue to try. Although we failed with you, Moshe – we succeeded after all. You taught us a lesson about life, that only someone who survived as a POW in German captivity, the Mezritch Ghetto, the *actzias*, Maidanek and Auschwitz, Buna and Buchenwald – only he knows how to teach.

You taught us the wisdom of life, to have sharp wits, to be cunning, not to be deceptive or loathsome in a way that is commonplace, but to be crafty, fair, to be full of incentive and sacrifice. And never to gain at the expense of others, even if they behaved to you quite the contrary. To be a man of values, integrity, righteous, an advocate of good, an advocate of peace.

83 years you lived in this hard world – a productive person, a creative person, with drive. Modestly, quietly, without complaining. A man who labored, a worker, a proletariat. A month and a half ago, as the disease nested deeply within you, you still went to work. A man of 83 who had to awake every morning to his daily labor, as is written: "Because every man is born to labor". The meaning of labor in the Torah is suffering. But you – work is pure joy for you, and you experience suffering only when you feel the lack desire.

Go in peace, Moshe. Take care of the sun for us up there, especially since it is declining on us lately. Perhaps a fuse really burned-out, or God – if you believe in him and of him a little – regrets the work of his hand that brought no pride. You in fact know the work...

Go in peace, Moshe. Very sad that you are not here, so happy that you were here. So you should remain. Go in peace.

One the eve of the outbreak of the Second World War the beautiful population of Mezritch numbered 18,000 Jews. At the Holocaust's end only 179 survived. The generation is dwindling. Today the remaining refugees are lacking one more survivor.

Prisoner 127942, Moshe Brezniak.
Go in peace.

Micha Friedman
Yarkon Cemetery; January 10, 2001

Appendix A: Notables

Actzia: An action, the Nazi round-up within Jewish population centers before mass deportation to the camps.

Aliyah: Literally: "to rise up", a term used by Jews to describe their immigration to Palestine, later the Israeli state; a spiritual metaphor.

Blockaltesta: A Kapo in charge of a block of prisoners' living quarters

Brezniak: Moshe's family name, the Polish word for a birch tree grove.

Commando: Prisoners of one specialty or professional group.

Eretz Yisrael: The Hebrew for "The Land of Israel", a name used by active Zionists.

Hashomer Hatzair: A Zionist youth group practicing a socialist orientation.

Judenrat: The Jewish constable force during the occupation, controlled by the Gestapo.

Kapo: Prisoner policemen who kept order in the camps, usually Jewish.

Mezritch: Miedzyrzec in Polish, meaning "the junction between two rivers". The Krzna (pronounced Kshena) River played a significant role for many survivors from town: for pre-war Shabbat strolls along the river and over the bridge, for summer swims that both Moshe and Mordechai enjoyed, and for poignant last-minute escapes from death.

Partisans: The local underground in Poland and elsewhere who fought the Nazis irregularly

Selectzia: The selection of Jews, the infamous choice between life and death made by an SS officer at central transfer points.

Zakoof: The Hebrew word for erect, upright, tall, proudly standing.

zloty: The Polish currency.

Printed in Great Britain
by Amazon

36503981R00142